# Closer to You: Lee

*Published by Phaze Books*
*Also by Marie Rochelle*

*All the Fixin'*

*My Deepest Love: Zack*

*Caught*

*Loving True*

*Taken By Storm*

*A Taste of Love: Richard*

*Taken by Storm*

*Cincinnati, Ohio*

# *Closer to You: Lee*

A novel of sensual romance by

# MARIE ROCHELLE

*Cincinnati, Ohio*

A Phaze Production
Phaze Books
6470A Glenway Avenue, #109
Cincinnati, OH 45211-5222
Phaze is an imprint of Mundania Press, LLC.

To order additional copies of this book, contact:
books@phaze.com
www.Phaze.com

Cover art © 2008 Debi Lewis
Edited by Amanda Faith

Trade Paperback ISBN-13: 978-1-60659-043-0

First Print Edition – November, 2008
Printed in the United States of America

10 9 8 7 6 5 4 3 2 1

This book is for everyone who fell in love with Lee. Enjoy.

Marie

# Chapter One

"Do you know why Mr. Cane called this meeting with everyone?" Missy Payne asked the woman sitting to her left.

Cherise Roberts looked at the perky brunette and wondered for the fifth time why she sat beside the chatty younger woman. She had been working at Cane's Marketing firm a little over six months now. Missy was like her shadow, and that was the only bad part about the job. Although Cherise hated to admit it, she was enjoying her new job. Yet, occasionally the antique shop did cross her mind.

However, she had owned the antique business for over five years and it had been time for her to move on. Being back in an office environment wasn't that bad; all the other employees had been nice enough to her.

"I don't know why he called this meeting. I think we'll find out when he's ready to come in and tell us," Cherise replied with impatience.

"I hope when I get to be your age, I'll have the intellect you do," Missy snickered, trying to insult her.

Cherise threw Missy a quick glance, stunned by the girl's disrespect. Several employees at the table heard what Missy said and waited to see how she was going to reply. They all knew how vocal and opinionated she was. "Thank you so much for the compliment," she replied through clenched teeth.

"But I never had the intelligence problem you do, so I don't think you'll ever end up like me. Sorry, Missy," Cherise added with a smirk to her full pouty lips. Loud laughter came from several people at the table. She didn't doubt that they silently agreed with her. Missy didn't get the job at Cane's Marketing for her cognitive skills.

"Yeah, but we all know the reason you got the job, don't we?" Missy shot back. Gathering up her pad and pencil, Missy moved away from her and found a new seat beside another employee at the conference room table.

Shaking off Missy's comment, Cherise opened her black journal and jotted down several ideas for the event she was catering this weekend. Since losing the antique shop to her brother-in-law, she decided to take up this new hobby. The idea really came from Traci, her baby sister, who had a birthday party for her husband two months ago.

The dinner turned out to be a smashing success, with Zack praising the food. Traci had asked her to cook for a small cocktail party. At first, she had turned her sister down saying her cooking was for fun, not profit. However, Traci had handed her a nice sized check and she had agreed. Cherise remembered all the problems Traci went through with Zack until they finally worked things out and got married.

Admitting she was wrong about Zack had been the hardest thing she had ever done in her life. Dating outside your race was hard enough. However, to marry a white man only made the problems two times harder on a couple. Cherise hadn't wanted Traci going through a lot of emotional drama while going to medical school to become a doctor. She had breezed through her college classes and now with the help of a tutor, Traci was handling the more difficult ones. She was woman enough to admit that Zack had turned out to be her sister's Prince Charming.

Now, she not only had him as a brother-in-law, but also gained three more: Richard, Brad, and Lee. When thoughts of Lee passed through her mind, Cherise tried to chase them away as quickly as possible, Lee Drace was her living and breathing nightmare of a *temptation* she didn't need in her life.

* * * *

Lee Drace towered over her at a massive six feet six inches. His watchful eyes were mixture of gray and green, with hints of blue thrown in to make her heart race every time they landed on her. She was constantly telling herself and him that the sight of him made her sick, but it was a lie. He was the most incredible-looking man to ever cross her path. Yet, why did he have to be in the wrong package? Sure, it was okay for Traci to fall in love with a white man and marry him. However, she didn't need any added pressures in her life.

However, Lee wasn't taking her screaming no at him all the time as an answer. Every time he saw her, they would end up in a room alone with his lips on hers. Hell, he knew how to kiss a sister until her knees went weak. But she would never tell him that because he was already self-centered.

He thought the world revolved around him and his every whim. *Maybe he had a right to be*, her mind thought. Out of all the brothers, Lee did have it all. He was the most successful, with Zack being a right on his heels. He was truly the total package and then some. *Stop thinking about him or you might give in to him one of these days when he asks you out again.*

Lee had been asking her out since the day Traci married his brother. Her usual answer was, "No, I don't date men in my family."

She would never forget how he answered her. They had been on vacation with Traci, Zack and the other brothers as a family getting to know each other thing. Somehow, she had gotten the pleasure of being left alone with Lee while everyone else went out sightseeing. They were the only ones by a secluded pool with him wearing only a pair of black swim shorts showing off his washboard stomach. Lee, the devil that he was, had slid his lounge chair next to her until not an inch separated them.

Lee had tried to coax her into the pool while his fingers stroked her bare arm. He promised that no one was looking at her body but him. She had told him for the sixth time no to the pool idea. There was no way her plus-sized body was getting into the pool wearing a swimsuit, not even one that she didn't mind wearing. The suit had been purchased out of a catalog and did a wonderful job hiding all the bad spots she wanted to hide from the public eye.

Well, Lee had gone on for another ten minutes until he figured out she wasn't getting into the pool with him. So, then conversation had lead to other things like his second favorite topic, their first date.

They had been out before but only as in-laws of the bride and groom. Lee wanted a real date for just the two of them. His wonderful colored eyes had slowly traveled up the length of her body to meet hers waiting with anticipating for her answer.

She had turned her head slightly, saying they would never go out on a date without the rest of the family. Lee's usual response would be to laugh and make a light joke. However, that time he kissed her quickly before she knew what was coming. Lee's moist firm mouth demanded a response from hers. A response she wasn't ready to give to him or even answer herself. Closing her eyes, Cherise could feel the heat of the kiss they shared by the pool.

Opening her eyes, Cherise cursed silently. Even in remembrance, she felt the intimacy of his kiss and his lips were more persuasive than she cared to admit. A woman could only take so much alone time with Lee Drace before his sex appeal started to wear her down. The door opening brought Cherise's attention back to the room and the reason they were all called in here today.

Justin Cane, their boss, walked in holding a thick file folder He tossed it on the boardroom table in front of her and waited for everyone to finish talking so he could speak.

"Good morning, everyone," his deep voice said. Taking his seat, Justin smiled before continuing. "I know people are wondering why I called this meeting this morning. So I'll make it as quick and painless as possible."

"I'm playing along with the idea of hiring another person to freelance with one of you here. Because I need more time to deal with some personal problems, I won't be able to spend much time in the office in the next couple of months."

"So, I need someone to sit in for me on meetings and report back to me as I work from home." Holding up his hand, he stopped two or three people from talking at once. "I know several of you would love to have the extra money, but I have picked out my three candidates to apply for the job. All the information you need is right here in these folders," he said tapping them with one finger. "After I have called the three people's names, the rest of you can leave for lunch."

Flipping one file over, Justin called out David Carlton's name, one the highest paid marketing assistants at the firm. The next person he mentioned was Missy Payne, who in the last few months had closed a lot of big deals.

Cherise wasn't really paying a lot of attention to what was going on around her. Her mind was on the party she had to cater this weekend and there were several things on her list that still needed to be done.

Traci was busy with the baby now and couldn't help her, but Cherise loved her little nephew so much. He looked so much like both of his parents. She was brought out her trance when Justin's tanned hand placed a file under her nose. Picking up the folder, she examined it more closely. It had her name in bold print across the front.

"Congratulations David, Missy, and Cherise. These are the three people I have chosen to compete for the assignment," Justin informed everyone. "I should also tell the three candidates that I won't be picking the winner, but the person I have hired will."

Justin stood up and was about to leave when Missy's voice stopped him. "Can you at least tell us more about the mystery person?" she asked.

With his hand on the doorknob, Justin looked at her and replied, "That would ruin the surprise and defeat the purpose of the competition." Opening the door, he went out and closed it with a loud click behind him.

Seconds later, other people at the meeting started clearing out of the room, too. Cherise sat there in shock that Mr. Cane even wanted her in the running for the job. She hadn't been here that long to showcase her talent.

"I don't know why you got picked to do this," Missy complained. "But I'm going to beat the both of you," she said, throwing out a direct challenge.

David shook his head sadly at Missy and left the room fast, but Cherise got stuck with hearing her whine. "Don't think Mr. Cane will let you have this to fill a quota," she hissed before strutting out of the room.

Staying in the boardroom, Cherise flipped opened the file looking down at what needed to be done for the competition. Why Mr. Cane decided to choose her for this task she would never know.

Shutting the folder, she decided to look over this better later on when she had more time. Picking up her journal along with the file, Cherise turned off the lights in the conference room and headed back to her office and the salad she had waiting for her inside the refrigerator.

During the last three months, she had dropped about ten pounds from her ultra curvy, plus-sized body. Now she knew that she would never look like her sister, but maybe with the ten pounds gone more guys would approach her. *I already have a guy who wants to approach me along with doing a whole lot more,* she thought. Lee didn't seem to have a problem with her curves every time his large hands roamed her body.

The first time his fingers traced her body was at the antique shop. Being totally surprised by his move, she didn't do anything but stand there. Lee Drace was a powerful force trying to break down her beliefs, but he didn't know how much stronger her will was. Finally making it to her office door, Cherise went inside to think about the competition and the new catering business she was trying to start at the same time. All the thoughts of the overly handsome Lee Drace was pushed to the back of her mind, at least for now.

\* \* \* \*

"You're one lucky man," Lee told his brother, handing his nephew back. "He's doesn't look anything like you."

Zack placed the baby securely in the car seat before answering him and covered his son with a light blanket. "Your sense of humor is going to get you in trouble," he teased, taking a bite of French toast.

Lee wiped his mouth, tossing it on the napkin on his plate. "How are things going at work? Is Tyshawn still pissed over having to work longer hours now?"

Zack had taken off for the last three weeks to help Traci with the baby while she studied for her finals. In the next couple of weeks, there would be a doctor in the family; Lee knew how proud Zack was of his wife. "No, he got over it towards the end of the week," Zack said while looking down at his son. "How's Brad doing?"

"We aren't talking that much right now," Lee replied with a sigh.

"Are the two of you still arguing over his feelings for Alicia Hart?" Zack asked, finishing off the last bite of his French toast.

"You know I don't think she's right for him," Lee said. "Brad has always been the protector of little lost things since he was a boy. Now he has this gorgeous woman he thinks needs to be taken care. I don't trust her. He's confusing protection with love."

Zack didn't want to get into this discussion with Lee because they always ended up on the wrong side.

Relaxing back in the sturdy chair, Zack watched his oldest brother for any signs of what his mind was thinking. He knew that Lee had been working on the freelance job plus other smaller things to bring in more business for the marketing firm. It wasn't like the business needed anymore money or press, because it was just listed in the top business magazine last week.

His brother had always been very successful when it came to his job and love life. But right now, the *love* life part was taking a nose dive with this new woman in his life Amanda Green. She was slowly driving his brother crazy with her needy ways. "Why are you dating Amanda when you want Cherise?"

Lee hardened at the mention of Traci's sexy older sister. Cherise kept him hot and bothered from the second he knew her name. But that damn willpower of hers kept them apart. "Don't let her name leave your mouth again," he yelled, waking up Carter.

Zack threw him a hard look. "You need to calm down."

"Sorry, I didn't mean to disturb the little guy," Lee apologized looking over at the baby. "It's just she makes me so furious," he said in a lower voice. "Cherise knows there's this potent attraction sizzling between us. Yet, she won't even go out on one date with me. Hell, what harm would one date cause?"

Laughing softly, Zack got up from the table and picked up the car seat. "You sound like I did when I was trying to get Traci to love me."

Lee's neck snapped around quickly. "I didn't say anything about being in love with Cherise."

"Keep telling yourself that," Zack laughed as he headed out the door.

Looking down, Lee noticed his brother had left Carter's baby bag. Snatching it up, he ran outside after Zack. "You forgot this." Standing behind Zack, Lee waited while he strapped his nephew in the back seat.

"Thanks. Can you toss it in the front seat?" Zack said looking over his shoulder.

Lee tossed the bag in the front seat and waited for Carter to be secured in the back, then resumed the conversation. "Don't go home and tell your wife than I'm in love with her sister."

Resting his arm on the car door, Zack relaxed his weight on it. "You're up against a losing battle, big brother. Keep surrounding yourself with all the useless relationships you want, but in the end the feelings you have for Cherise will bring you back to her."

"Whatever you do, don't hurt Cherise," he threatened. "She has this tough untouchable attitude. Yet, she has so much caring for the other people around her that you would never think it was her. I was stunned when I found out how caring she was," Zack admitted to his baffled brother. "Not once has she brought up the past since I married Traci. She has been a wonderful sister-in-law and I won't let you use her and toss her to the side when you are finished."

Lee was amazed how Zack was sticking up for Cherise. "Are you forgetting that I'm your brother?" Lee questioned as Zack slid in the car closing the door.

"Yeah, that's why I'm telling you to not play around with Cherise."

Moving back, Lee watched his brother pull out of the long driveway, waving goodbye out of window.

Later in the afternoon, Lee was working from home trying to put the final touches on his newest business deal. He enjoyed working at the office. But staring at the walls was getting a little boring day in and day out. He missed the excitement of working on a new project from beginning to end.

Reclining back in the leather chair, Lee thought back to when he was younger and first started up his business. It had been right out of college. The work had been very hard, but by the time he turned twenty-six, there was a nice amount of money in his bank account. God, he missed the thrill of chasing a dream!

A light knock at the door drew his attention. "Come on in," Lee yelled at the other person standing on the outside and picked up his pen at the same time. Amanda Green walked into the room. Her mile-long legs looked captivating in a pair of black four-inch heels with her long sandy-blonde hair swinging between her shoulder blades. Not one ounce of fat was on her perfectly toned body, which for some reason upset him. *What happened to the time a woman wasn't a bag of bones?*

"Hello, Lee. What are you doing tomorrow night?" she asked moving behind the chair wrapping her slender arms around his neck.

"Amanda, I don't want to do anything while I'm working on this business deal. You know I have told you this," Lee's deep voice pointed out, weary of Amanda's attempts to get him back into her bed.

Pouting, Amanda took the pen from his hand, tossing it on the desk. She spun him around and sat down on his lap. "Lee, I'm having this big dinner party tomorrow to unveil one on my client's new paintings. I want you there with me."

Sighing, Lee threw his head on the back of the seat. "Amanda, you know how much I hate those art gathering parties. All of your clients are so superficial around me. I don't think one of them even likes the sight of me there with you."

Dating a woman who was an art dealer had turned out to be a bad idea for him and now he couldn't find a way out without hurting her feelings. It wasn't as fun as he thought it would be. Besides, he only started dating Amanda to get his mind off Cherise.

"Oh, baby," she pouted. "You're so wrong. All my friends love you. Didn't I tell you that one even wanted to use you as a nude model for her art class?"

Lee couldn't imagine posing naked in front of class of twelve students. He wasn't shy about his body, but that was a little too much even for him to handle. "Remember I told you no," he answered, sliding Amanda off his lap and standing. "You did tell her I said no?" he asked, looking down at Amanda.

"Yes, I told Leslie what you said, but she was very disappointed," Amanda answered. "If I promise not to drag you to another art gallery or museum for the next three months, will you be my date?" she asked.

"Lady, you have a deal!" Lee agreed because he hated going to the museum more than one of Amanda's parties. Screaming, Amanda wrapped herself back in his arm planting a kiss on his lips.

\* \* \* \*

This was the night of her first big party and Cherise was having a melt down because there were more people out there than first expected. Like always, she had made extra, but what if it wasn't enough and the hostess wanted all the money back. This wasn't happening to her. Calming herself down, Cherise went over the menu one more time in her head. The finger foods were on the table placed on shiny sliver trays. She had decided to go with puff pastry pretzels and Gougeres with crab salad after the hostess had mention how much all her friends liked those two things. Both hors d'oeuvres looked delicious and smelled even better.

16

Walking up to one of the waitresses, Cherise told her to take the first tray out while she finished working on the puff pastry pretzels. Nodding, the young girl walked through the door out into the crowded room. Ten minutes later, a tray of pretzels was out there, too. Checking on the side dish inside the oven, she made sure it was warming up nicely. She had already looked at the main course along with the desserts and they both looked mouth-watering.

Taking off her apron, she moved around the huge kitchen making sure there was enough of everything just in case something happened. This party had to go perfectly so Amanda Green would recommend her to another client. It felt good to have another job on the side for fun. The cooking wasn't hard, because it had been a love of hers for years. Knowing this may be the only free time she would get, Cherise decided to make a quick bathroom break.

* * * *

Out in the main room, Lee popped another mouth-watering crab puff into his mouth. He savored how flaky and good the fresh crabmeat tasted. Whoever fixed these had a talent that was probably worth more than Amanda was paying them. He had been bored since he stepped foot in the huge loft apartment.

At least Amanda had good taste, the place was decorated as only an art dealer could do. Looking to his left, he saw a smiling Amanda working the room as she usually did, wearing a very low cut dress for her rich male buyers. The more paintings the artist sold, the more money put into Amanda's bank account. Walking around, he tried to find more crab puffs, but the servers only had the pretzel pastries that were good, but not as excellent as the crab.

Knowing his date would be in a conversation for a while before she missed him, Lee sneaked into the kitchen. Moving around the large area, he was about to give up hope on finding anymore crab until he saw a tray sitting by the stove. From the looks of them, they just came out of the oven. Lee walked over and popped a warm one in his mouth.

Swallowing it down, Lee licked his lips savoring the wonderful taste. As his hand reached for another crab treat a sexy voice spoke behind him, "Sir, if you go back out to the party. I'll send the tray out by one of the servers."

Placing the puff on a napkin next to the tray, Lee thought the voice sound very familiar. He turned around slowly and his eyes connected with Cherise's. He grinned at the stunned look that passed over her gorgeous face. This night was going to turn out *better* than he first thought.

"Hello, sexy," he said walking closer to her. His eyes stripping the green wrap around dress from her tempting body. "Are you the one catering this party?" he asked standing so near now that Cherise could feel his breath on her cheek.

*No,* Cherise's mind screamed. Lee isn't standing in front of her looking so handsome in his black suit. I can't be caught in here with him alone. It would be another five minutes before any of the servers came back in for another tray. Her body would betray her in two minutes if Lee touched her, let alone pressed those firm lips of his on hers.

"Lee, what are you doing here?" Cherise asked, trying to move around him, but Lee placed his arm on the table blocking her in.

"I know you won't answer me until I answer you," he said reaching out to touch her shorter hair. "Why did you cut your hair? I liked the way it brushed your breasts when you wore it down."

Gasping at his intimate talk, Cherise leaned back from him. "You didn't answer my question," she whispered looking at his mouth.

Lee noticed her eyes on him and it made his body respond. "I'm friends with Amanda Green and she needed a date," he answered, running the pad of his thumb over the pulse beating in her neck.

Cherise didn't believe any man would be just friends with a woman who looked like Amanda. "Sure, you're just friends with Amanda and I just won the lottery," Cherise snapped, pushing at his chest so he would move.

Was that jealousy he heard in her voice? He was ecstatic because if she was showing this kind of interest in him, maybe it would lead to more things. "Cherise, are you going to answer my question?" Lee whispered in her ear.

The feel of his breath on her earlobe made Cherise's eyes close for an instant and then reopen them. "Yes, I'm working here at the party," she responded looking into his beautiful eyes. God, why did he have to be everything she wanted but in the wrong package? Traci found her prince, but Lee Drace would never be hers because she wouldn't allow it.

"Could you please move so I can check on the food?" she asked, her hand touching him in the middle of the chest.

Lee always lost his train of thought when Cherise touched him. "I'll move on one condition."

"I'm not going to kiss you," she muttered.

Running his fingers through her shoulder length pageboy haircut, Lee cupped her chin in his hand making her look him in the eye. "I don't want a kiss, yet, but I will get one in the future," he promised his mouth inches from hers.

Licking her lipstick-covered mouth, Cherise asked, "What do you want from me?"

Easing his hand down her back, he cupped her firm butt. Yanking her to his aroused body, he brushed his lower body slowly against her making a gasp ease between her lips. "A date," he said, staring into her eyes.

Her eyes widened in fear. To go out on a date with Lee would be committing suicide to her mind, body, and soul. He was way too devilish to ignore. "I can't," Cherise answered trying to get out of his light yet strong hold.

"Why not?" he asked, forcefully.

"Let go of me," she said squirming in his hold, the feel of him through her thin dress was driving her crazy.

"Not until you tell me why," he replied, pressing her body completely to his.

Biting her lips, she looked into his eyes again. "I can't tell you, Lee," her soft voice whispered. Sinful eyes widened then narrowed with anger.

Picking her up, Lee carried her into the bathroom that he knew was to the left of him. He closed and locked the door behind them.

She gasped at how quickly Lee moved with her weight. "You picked me up," she whispered as he sat her on the vanity in the large bathroom.

"Don't start with me about your weight," he growled. "Are you dating someone?"

Shoving at his chest, Cherise got him to move back from her. "How dare you ask me that? You're dating Amanda, which means you have no claim on me," Cherise informed him hotly.

Moving quickly, Lee pressed her back against the mirror with his large body, "I'm not dating Amanda, she's dating me," Lee said.

# *Chapter Two*

Taking her finger, Cherise poked Lee hard in the chest. "You're a liar, Lee Drace," her soft voice rung out in the empty bathroom. "I don't want to be around you unless I have to. Now move out of my way," she snapped, shoving him hard.

Lee knew by the look in her eyes that he had made a mistake with her. "We need to talk about some things."

Sliding off the vanity, Cherise unlocked the door and stormed out in the kitchen just in time to hear the timer go off. Sitting the roast pork with sage and garlic on the counter, she heard Lee come out of the bathroom. She felt his eyes looking at her, but she refused to look at him.

"I'm not giving up on getting that date from you, sweetheart," he whispered before going out the door.

* * * *

The rest of the night went by without any problems or anymore visits from Lee. Everyone at the party loved the fresh cream of pea soup as a side dish and the main course of the roast pork with sage and garlic went over fantastic. By the end of the night, everyone was enjoying the open bar, while the cleaning crew she hired took care of the last items.

"Ms. Roberts," Amanda Green said, coming in the kitchen with the check in her hand.

"Yes?" Cherise said, putting on her coat as she got ready to leave. She was delighted because her purse was full of numbers of potential new clients.

"I paid you a little more for the wonderful job you did," Amanda commented handing her the check.

Smiling, Cherise slid the check into her pocket. "Thank you. I'm glad everything was to your liking."

"I hope you keep up your business because I might need you for my wedding in the future," Amanda grinned.

Feeling her heart drop to the bottom of her stomach, Cherise asked, "You're getting married?"

"I would love to, if I could ever convince my boyfriend to take that big walk down the aisle."

Cherise pushed down her hurt at the thought of Lee marrying the woman in front of her. It was none of her business. He could do what he wanted with his life. "Well, I wish you luck." Picking up her purse, she walked out of the kitchen and went to the elevator. She was so lost in her thoughts that she didn't notice Lee, standing to the side, looking at her with a watchful expression.

The elevator doors opened and Cherise walked inside ready to get home and take a long hot bubble bath. As the doors were about to shut, a hand reached out and stopped them. Looking at the door, she watched Lee get inside with her. "What in the hell are you doing?" she asked, spinning around to face him as the door slid closed.

Pressing the down button, Lee rested his back against the wall taking in how truly beautiful Cherise was with her tawny eyes and rich brown skin. He still wasn't pleased that she cut most of her hair off, but the new haircut was very attractive. "I thought I would walk my sister-in-law to her car," he said, smiling at her.

Butterflies came into her stomach when Lee flashed her that boyish smile he loved using when he wanted something.

"I can make it to my car just fine without your help," she replied, folding her arms moving slightly away from him.

"Let me be a gentleman for you," he said, easing closer to her.

From the corner of her eyes, Cherise took how hunky her brother-in-law was. She didn't like being in small areas with him because it made the chemistry between them so much harder to deny. "Won't your girlfriend get upset you left without saying goodbye?" Cherise questioned arching her eyebrow.

"Amanda isn't my girlfriend and what I do with my own time is my damn business," he said, brushing her thick hair back from her cheek.

"Stop touching me. You know I've told you that several times," Cherise muttered, as she removed his hand from her face.

"I'm a man that enjoys touching beautiful things," he admitted with a wink.

Laughing, she moved away until her back was pressed to the wall and she could look directly at his face. "You have a way with words that any man would envy," she whispered. "Or should I say empty words?"

Lee's eyes blinked at the sarcastic tone of Cherise's voice. "I mean the words I say to you, darling," he confessed. "I think you are one of the most amazing looking women I have ever seen."

She stared wordlessly at him; he seemed so sincere. However, when Lee wanted something, he knew how to throw on the charm. Shaking her head, Cherise chuckled at him. "Is that the line you used on Amanda that made her fall in love with you?" she inquired. "Do you know that she asked me to caterer her wedding?"

Lee's stiffen as the words came out of her mouth. "Who is she marrying?"

"Why you," she replied, pointing at him with a smirk.

Lee's face paled at the thought of being married to Amanda and hearing all the useless chatter from her and all the people she hung around. "When did she tell you we were getting married?" he asked, truly taken aback.

"When she handed me the extra check for the excellent job I did at the party." Cherise wondered why the elevator was taking so long getting them to the parking lot. She hadn't wanted to be alone in here with him, but it would have rude to walk off when he got on. She couldn't ignore him now, because he was part of the family.

"I'm not getting married to her," Lee reiterated, trying to get her to believe him.

"Hey, you don't have to explain anything to me," Cherise said while searching her purse. Sshe pulled out a calendar and tried to avoid any further conversation with Lee. The less she talked to him, the better.

Flipping through it, Cherise noticed she didn't have another party, which was a theme party, scheduled for weeks. It would give her more than three weeks to plan it. Researching what to serve was going to be a huge part of this catering job, plus it was paying her three times her usual price. She wanted it to be excellent.

Lee noticed how Cherise was trying to pretend he wasn't in the same space with her, but he wasn't going to let her to it. "I thought you had found another job through a person Traci knew at the hospital."

Placing the calendar back in the purse, Cherise gave him a heated look. "Are you checking up on me?" she questioned.

Lee knew he didn't have to right to ask Traci about her, but sometimes he couldn't help it. She drew him faster than any other woman from his past. "Well, you're a part of my family now, so I have to know what's going on it your life," he said trying to find a way out.

Amazed at the thrill that shot through her body, Cherise kept any expressions off her face. She didn't want Lee to know how his words made her feel. He was interested in what was going on her in life, but she didn't let it show on her face.

Why was he talking to Cherise when they were alone in an empty quiet elevator? There were so many other fun things they could be doing with their mouths. Moving swiftly, he pressed Cherise's body to the far corner, covering her mouth swiftly with his.

The kiss was slow and thoughtful, allowing her time to pull back if she wanted to, but he was praying hard that she wouldn't. His tongue explored the recesses of her mouth, tasting the mint and tea from earlier, growling he licked the roof of her mouth. Pulling her body hard to his aroused body, Cherise gasped in his mouth at the feel of his cock poking her in the stomach.

The kiss sent the pit of her stomach into a wild whirlwind resembling a tornado. Giving herself freely to the passion of his kiss, she stood on tiptoe wrapping her arms around Lee's strong shoulders. Feeling her breasts pressed into his chest sent Lee over the edge.

Lifting her up, he laid her down on the elevator floor. "Baby, you feel so damn hot beneath me," he moaned, sliding his hand between Cherise's warm thighs, stroking lightly. The hotness of her skin burned at his long fingers. As he was about to touch her underwear with his fingers, the elevator stopped, shocking both of them.

Jerking Cherise up before the doors opened, he placed her on one side and moved quickly to the other, just as the doors slid open. Luckily, there wasn't anyone waiting to get in or the sexual tension would have eaten the person alive.

Shocked by her behavior, Cherise ran to her car, ignoring Lee as he screamed her name. She got in, slammed the door and took off down the tunnel.

"Shit," Lee cursed as Cherise's headlights faded off. He wondered how in the hell he was going to fix this mess.

\* \* \* \*

"You can work as hard as you want, but you aren't going to win this deal," Missy said, coming into Cherise's office and collapsing on the leather couch the next day.

Without looking up, Cherise replied, "Don't you have someone else to bother today or is it my lucky day?"

"Why are you such a bitch?" Missy hissed.

Slowly, Cherise's eyes looked up from the report. "Don't ever call me that again, Missy," she stated in a deadly calm voice.

Sighing, Missy stood up, pulling at her short white skirt that matched her jacket. "I just said what everyone else thinks about you. So, I don't know why you got mad at me." Strutting out the door, she tossed back over her shoulder, "I thought you liked honesty."

"She's trying to mess with your mind," David said, coming to stand in the open doorway. "Yesterday, Missy came into my office saying I wouldn't get the job because looking like the boy next door wouldn't help me."

A smile lit up her face at the only person she could get along with at the office, which surprised her because David wasn't black, but white. Maybe accepting Zack into the family has opened up her mind to more friends than just black ones.

"Close that door and have a seat," she said, gesturing towards the seat in front of her.

Looking out the door to make sure no one else was paying attention, David closed the door and walked over to her. Sitting down on the edge of her desk, he crossed his arms over his chest. "Do you have any idea who we will be working with?"

David didn't like surprises in his business or personal life. He planned everything down to what he was going to have for breakfast, lunch, and dinner for the next day. Cherise thought her co-worker was so funny and cute. He had a way of making her laugh.

"I have something for you," she said. Reaching underneath her desk, she pulled out a medium-sized white bag out of the refrigerator she kept there. "I had some extra crab puffs left over along with those pretzels you love so much," she said, handing him the sack.

"I knew I became friends with you for a reason," David laughed. He took the bag from her and stood up. "This is going home with me. I can have it for dinner. Mary is going away on a business trip. You know Mary still wants to fix you up with a guy from her job."

Cherise doubted Mary mentioned the extra weight she was carrying around. "I have told you that I don't have much extra time for dating."

She could tell from the look on David's face he wasn't going to take no for an answer this time. "Sorry, you are not backing out this time, Ms. Roberts," he said. "As soon as Mary gets back in town, we are all going out on a double date."

Glaring at David, Cherise saw no amount of begging was going to make him change his mind. "Well, you have to let me know in head of time, so the date won't be the same time I'm catering a party. I think I have about twelve more to do before the year is out," she said, writing down a note on her desk calendar to double check dates and make phone calls to the clients.

"Are you sure you aren't spreading yourself too thin?" he asked, concerned about his friend, because she had a really bad perfection complex. Everything had to be done a certain way before she gave up and moved on. "Remember, you have to work on the assignment Mr. Cane gave us two days ago."

She already had plans to start working on it tonight at home. Each night she had been making an outline how she was going to do the report, but she doubted the winner would be her. "You know that you're going to win this," she teased David, who was moving toward the door to leave.

"I really don't have time to be working on a new assignment now," he groaned, still mad he had gotten chosen in the first place.

"What? Why not? You love working on stuff like this," she said surprised.

David flashed a grin. "I don't have time to go into it now. But later today, I'll make it back here and tell you about my future plans." He shut the door behind him as he left her office.

\* \* \* \*

With the office quiet and empty now, Cherise's mind wandered back to what happened last night at the party with Lee. *How in the hell did I let him do those things to me?* God, in the past she always had control over her body, but when he was around all the common sense her mother stressed to her left her body. *Why did his kisses have to be so potent?* That man could make a sister forget all about her dreams and run away with him at the drop of a hat. Damn, she wouldn't allow him within twenty feet of her anymore.

Luckily, her nights were filled with planning her next catering event and working on getting this report done by the end of the month. Both of those things should keep her very busy and her mind off her ultra hot brother-in-law. Pushing him to the back of her mind, Cherise picked up the file that Mr. Cane wanted to talk to her about.

Making her way from her office to his, she saw Missy inside her office working hard. It had to be on the new marketing project she just received. Cherise had really wanted to work with that company, but they wanted someone more perky and young, so she had lost out on the account.

Shaking off this disappointment, she kept walking until she came to Justin Cane's office door. Knocking once, she waited for him to answer it.

"Come in."

Opening the door, Cherise walked in. "Good morning, Mr. Cane," she said, closing the door behind her.

"Good morning, Ms. Roberts," Justin said, placing his coffee cup back down on his desk.

"Hello, sir," Cherise replied back, showing her boss some respect. She was the only one at the marketing firm that didn't call him by his first name.

"Please have a seat," he said, standing up waiting for her to take a seat.

"Thank you, sir," Cherise said, taking the seat he had offered.

"How has your day been so far?" he asked, retaking his seat.

"I can't complain," she replied, holding the file in her hand.

"Did I hear you started a catering business?" Justin asked, wanting to know more about his newest employee.

With a smile, Cherise told Mr. Cane about her catering business, but left out the part about how she used to own an antique shop. Mr. Cane didn't need to know everything about her personal life. It was best to keep the private side of her life away from the office as much as possible. She wasn't the kind of woman who shared a lot about herself with co-workers.

"Here's the file that you wanted from me, Mr. Cane," Cherise said, laying it on his desk. Justin picked the file and looked over it while she waited for an answer.

"You have done a wonderful job on the account, Ms. Roberts," he praised, glancing up from the report. "I knew how disappointed you were when I didn't give you the shoe account that Missy is working on now."

Cherise couldn't keep the surprise off her face. "How did you know about that?"

"Yes, I thought you might be stunned that I knew about your reaction to that," Justin told her. "You handled it very well when I called her name instead of yours. However, I thought your talents would be better suited for the marketing account you just finished up and it seems that I was correct."

Justin thought very highly of Cherise. She was always on time and never complained about working extra hours if she had to. The only other employee he had like that was David, but David had been here longer than Ms. Roberts and knew how to work the office. Both were very intelligent and talented when it came to their jobs, but Cherise had an extra spark about it. It didn't come out all the time in her work, but when it did, the project turned out unbelievable.

"Have you started working on the project for the position assisting the freelance person I hired?" he asked, relaxing back in his chair.

"I'm going to start working on it tonight, because I don't have anymore catering jobs until next month," Cherise answered.

"Good, I wanted to make sure that everyone has enough time to get it in before the deadline."

She thought it was a good idea that Mr. Cane wasn't the one picking the winner so there wouldn't be any problem, but she did have a question for him. "Why did you pick me to compete in this when I have only been here six months?"

Justin wondered how long it would be before Cherise asked him that question. "Well, let me go down the list of reasons, Ms. Roberts. You're very dependable and reliable when it comes to getting things done. I know you're responsible and will stick with the project to the end no matter how hard it might become."

"Another reason is you're very efficient and consistent in the type of work that you do each and every time. I can tell you go over it thoroughly before handing it in," Justin praised. "How could I not let you be one of the top three people up for the account?" he asked, stunned.

It amazed Cherise that Mr. Cane had picked up on her personality so well after only knowing her for a short period of time.

"Looks like everyone is starting to leave for the today, so I'll talk to you later on in the week," he said, staring out his glass window into the hallway of the office. "Why don't you go ahead and leave, too?"

Telling Mr. Cane goodbye, Cherise left and headed back to her office. Tonight, she was supposed to have dinner with Traci and Zack, but she called and cancelled earlier saying she was busying working on an assignment. However, the real reason was she didn't want to run into Lee after the elevator incident. Traci had been hurt, but said she understood and rescheduled the dinner for next week.

She didn't think she was hiding from Lee at all. She was just avoiding making a bad situation worse. There was no way there would ever be anything between the two of them. He had a girlfriend that he kept trying to deny and she wasn't going to get involved with her sexier-than-sin brother-in-law.

\* \* \* \*

At the restaurant, Lee sat at table half listening to Amanda talk about a new artist she wanted to work for, because the conversations were always the same when it came to her. His mind was on other things that were more important. Like why Cherise had cancelled out on the dinner invitation with Traci and his brother. God, he wasn't going to attack her right there on the dining room table. Well, not his brother's dining room table anyway.

31

Cherise was still fighting their attraction even after the steaming scene they had in the elevator.

Why wouldn't she just give in and have one date with him? It would make it so much easier for her to agree to them being a couple. He still couldn't believe how his opinions about interracial dating changed the second that he saw her in the antique shop. Since then the only thought in his mind has been getting her to loosen up more and go out with him. The woman worked way too hard and didn't spend enough time out having fun.

He knew from talking with Traci that Cherise hadn't been on a date in over three years, which he found shocking. Cherise was so damn sexy. He had the hardest time keeping his hands off her when they were in a room together. However, being attracted to her wasn't the only reason he wanted to date her, her intelligence drew him more than her body. She had been the only woman in his life that could keep up with his dry sense of humor and come back with a comment of her own.

In addition, his size didn't intimate her in the least. Out of all his brothers, Lee knew he was the biggest. Yet, Cherise stood up to him like she was the same size. He loved the passion that always seemed to be burning in her body. Just one touch from her sent his body in overdrive. He needed a way to get near Cherise without it seeming like it was planned or him being overly dominating.

It was going to be a slow process to gain her trust, especially how he took the antique shop from her for his brother. She might have forgiven Zack because she wanted to keep Traci in her life, but Lee knew he was still on her bad side. It didn't matter how many times he stole a kiss or two from her.

The need to have Cherise around him was more powerful than before and the kisses only added fuel to his slow-burning fire. Most of the time women were the ones chasing him and he was thinking of a way to avoid them.

He didn't know if he liked being on the other side. Zack had told him that Cherise was only interested in dating black men.

*What if those times he had kissed her she was fantasizing about someone else?* Lee didn't like the thoughts coming into his mind. Cherise wanted him and he knew it. Now, he only needed to find a way to get her to admit her feelings, but for that to happen, they had to spend more time around each other. Maybe one of his brothers would have an idea. Lee was about to get up and leave when he realized he was on a date with Amanda.

"We need to leave," Lee told her, walking over pulling out her chair.

"Lee, your mind hasn't been on us since you picked me up," Amanda said walking out of the building with him. "Are you seeing someone else?" she asked.

He didn't want to hurt her feelings, because Amanda wasn't a bad woman, she just wasn't who he wanted anymore. Lee stopped walking and answered her question. "Amanda, you're a very sweet woman," his deep voice replied. "But I'm not interested in you that way and I think I started to date you trying to fill a void placed by someone else."

Amanda couldn't be upset by his confession because he had never promised her a silver lining. She kissed him lightly on the cheek. "I think I know who the lucky woman is," she confessed, moving back from him.

For a moment, he studied her intently, "You know who I'm trying to date?" he questioned.

"No, I know who you're in love with, Lee," Amanda answered, laughing at him.

Sliding his hands into his slacks, Lee looked at her long and hard. "Who am I in love with?"

There was a faint glint of humor in Amanda's eyes as she took in his defensive stance. "Cherise Roberts, the caterer from my party, and I believe she's also your sister-in-law," Amanda answered with a cute little smirk. "I had been hearing rumors from my friends about your attraction to her, but I saw it two nights again at my art showing. You couldn't take your eyes off her when she entered the room."

"Why do people keep telling me how I feel about Cherise?" Lee asked, frustrated. "I only want to date her," he said, shaking his dark head, not paying attention to the fact that Amanda was trying to get a cab.

Hailing a cab, Amanda opened the door. "No, you are in love with her. Remember, I'm an art dealer and I have an eye for these things."

Lee had been so caught in his own thoughts that he didn't notice Amanda by the opened cab door until now. "Wait, I'll give you a ride back home," Lee said, not wanting Amanda to take a cab back home. He brought her and he should take her back home.

"Don't worry about me. I can take care of myself, Lee," Amanda said, getting into the taxi. "Just send me an invitation to the wedding," she yelled out the window as the driver pulled away.

"I'm not in love with her," Lee kept muttering to himself as he went to his car.

\* \* \* \*

The same words were coming out of his mouth as he unlocked his front door and tossed his car keys on the antique table that he had someone buy for him when Cherise closed her business. She had no clue he even had it in his house or the other pieces he had upstairs in his bedroom.

To be in love with Cherise meant he wanted her in his personal space. He was quite comfortable with his life the way it was. Anytime he wanted to be spontaneous, he could without asking anyone's opinions about his choices. Not that he was impulsive all the time or anything, but there were rare occasions that he was.

Caring too deeply about his sister-in-law would change that part of him; Lee always knew what he was doing when it came to any physical or mental obstacle. He wasn't a man to doubt himself. Even as a little boy, he always knew what he wanted and getting married, having children or being deeply in love wasn't ever on his list. No, they were all wrong about him loving Cherise Roberts. Yet, she could handle any one-liner he threw her way. Even his brothers told him his humor wasn't appropriate for certain situations and he had to stop.

Lee made up his mind to ignore what people said around him and live his life the way he wanted. He found Cherise fascinating and very desirable, but those two things didn't add up to love. Tomorrow was a busy day for him. Richard wanted him to come by *D4* and Brad wanted to see him around two o'clock. His patience was wearing thin with his baby brother. Sure, Brad was starting to spend more time at the office; however, his mind was always filled with thoughts of that reporter, Alicia Hart.

Brad was always falling for a woman who didn't value his love. He needed to get the other brothers together so they could have a long talk with him. Pushing Brad out of his mind until he got the chance to speak with him, Lee wondered when he would see Cherise again. He knew it better be soon, because he craved another kiss from her.

# Chapter Three

Three days later, Cherise read over her marketing plan that was due back to Mr. Cane in an hour. All last week, she had stayed at work late typing it out. David told her Missy turned her plan in twenty minutes ago, and he gave his to Mr. Cane's secretary yesterday, so that just left her.

Flipping through it one last time, Cherise slid it into the manila envelope with the number three written across the top in black marker. Once the envelope was sealed, it wasn't going to be opened until it touched the proper hands. When the competition for this assignment first began, she didn't want to win. But the more time she put into it, the more important it became to win this one badly.

Leaving her workspace, Cherise walked to Mr. Cane's office and saw his secretary clearing off her desk to leave for the day. "Sorry, I didn't have it here sooner," Cherise apologized.

"Don't worry about it," she said taking the manila envelope from her sliding it into her purse. "Good luck," she told Cherise, touching her on the shoulder as she left the office.

On her way back to her desk, her cell phone started to ring. "Hello?"

"Hey, big sis," Traci's voice said on the other end.

"Traci," Cherise said with a smile in her voice. "I was wondering if you would mind having dinner with me and Carter tonight at my house. Zack's having his weekly brother dinner and I didn't want to go," Traci told her.

Cherise's heart sank a little at hearing Lee wouldn't be there and she didn't want to think why.

"Girl, you know I would love to have dinner with you and my adorable nephew," Cherise said. "I can bring the present by I brought him yesterday."

"Cherise, you can't get him anything else or we're going to have to make the nursery bigger," she teased.

Continuing on to her office while still on the phone with her sister, Cherise picked up her purse and turned off the light. "Can I help it if his mommy doesn't get him anything?" Cherise teased back. "That's what having an aunt is for," she said, coming out her office heading toward the exit. "Give me about thirty minutes and I'll be there," she told Traci, hanging up the phone as she left the building.

\* \* \* \*

Making two quick stops first, Cherise then headed to Traci's house on the upper side of town. It was a purchase Zack had made right before popping the question to Traci. After she said yes, he decided to fix it up and keep it for his family. She was truly happy that Traci had found love with Zack. Pulling into the driveway, Cherise got out of the car and walked right on in without knocking. She kept telling Traci to keep the front door locked; it didn't matter how nice the neighborhood was.

The first sound she heard was Carter crying. "What are you doing to my baby?" she asked Traci, looking at the crying baby in her sister's arms.

"I'm trying to feed him, but he doesn't want to take the bottle," Traci sighed.

"Give me Carter and I'll feed him," Cherise said, reaching for the baby.

Traci handed the fussy baby over to Cherise along with his bottle. Handing Traci her car keys, Cherise said, "Go and get those bags out of the front seat."

Sitting down at the kitchen table, Cherise gave the bottle to her adorable nephew Carter and he took it instantly. Traci stood there in shock a few minutes, then laughed as she went toward the front door. Unlocking the car door, Traci grabbed the two bags. Slamming the door shut and making sure it was locked, she ran back into the house. Her sister was still at the table feeding her son, who couldn't take his eyes off her.

"I think Carter loves his Aunt Cherise," Traci told her, placing the bags on the table.

"I should hope so after the present I brought for him," she said, pointing to the black bag on the table.

"What did you do?" Traci asked, sitting down at the table opening the bag. Lifting the lid off the shoebox, she pulled out a pair of baby Jordans and a matching outfit. "Cherise, you need to stop buying him all these expensive things," Traci scolded.

Sitting the empty bottle on the table, Cherise placed the baby on her shoulder patting his back softly and answered her sister. "What's the use of having a little extra money if you can't spend it on the ones you love?" Cherise asked, moving her nephew to the other shoulder. "Stop complaining and get dinner started," she teased her little sister. Getting up from the table, Cherise walked around the house with Carter, while Traci worked on their dinner.

Moving to the long hallway, Cherise looked at the family photos that Traci had hung on the wall. It took a lot of begging from Traci before she would ever take a picture for this wall. Who in their right mind would want to place her on the wall and then to place her next to her worst nightmare? Was she ever going to get away from him? Luckily, it had been days since she had seen him. She honestly hadn't missed him. Deep down, Cherise knew she was lying to herself. Lee did add some adventure to her stale life, yet she wasn't about to confess that to anyone. "Hey, why didn't you want to go to Lee's house?" she asked, coming back into the living room with the sleeping baby.

Traci stopped stirring the pot in the kitchen and came to the living area to answer her. "Let me take Carter. I'll change him and put him to bed and then I'll tell you." She left the room and headed to the nursery.

Going back into the kitchen and over to the stove, Cherise tasted the sauce and shook her head. "My sister doesn't know how to season her food at all," she mumbled to herself. Grabbing a spice off the spice rack by her shoulder, she tossed a few pinches in and with a quick stir, the sauce tasted better in an instant.

"I knew you couldn't resist fixing that sauce," Traci laughed, taking the plates out of the cabinet.

"Sorry," Cherise said, taking the plates from her. Setting the table, Cherise stopped and looked at Traci. "You look so happy," she said, more to her herself than to her sister.

"I'm very happy." Traci grinned, placing the food on the table. Looking at Cherise more closely, she saw the sadness in her sister's eyes and it pained her. "Cherise, what's wrong?" she asked worried.

"Oh, I'm fine," Cherise answered, plastering a fake smile on her face.

"Don't you dare lie to me Cherise Michelle Roberts," Traci snapped sounding like the older sister instead of the younger one. Pulling out a chair, she grabbed Cherise's arm and said, "Now, you sit down and tell me what has you so upset." She shoved her sister down in the chair and sat across from her. "That's why I stayed home tonight. We haven't had dinner alone in such a long time. I know you and something is wrong. Tell me.

* * * *

All the loneliness and confusion was twisting itself together inside her mind and heart. It had been so long since she knew how it felt to be around a man who cared about her. She was the kind of person who loved being in a relationship with the handholding and kissing to show affection to the other person. Cherise didn't know the last time she had been excited about a date or looked forward to hearing a man's on the other end of the phone.

With all the years she spent working at the antique shop, it didn't matter because it was there to fill her time. But now with Traci being married and having a new baby, she realized how empty her life truly was. However, she didn't want to bring down Traci's happiness.

Her sister had found everything she had been looking for in under a year. Yet in the last two years, no man had shown any interest in her and Lee wasn't even going to enter her mind as an option. Tormented by confusing emotions, Cherise still couldn't find the words to answer her sister.

*How can I tell my sister how lonely I am without upsetting her?* Sometimes misery needed to be kept to yourself and not forced onto another person; that included your family. She still had too much pride to allow Traci to know about her inner turmoil. A smile found its way to her mouth, although she was uncertain about her future.

"I'm worried about this account I have to compete for at work," Cherise lied. "It's a huge project and I really want it, but I'm up against David and Missy," she sighed. Traci didn't need to know the real reason for her mood. It wasn't like she could help with it anyway.

"God...Cherise, I thought maybe you were having man problems," Traci groaned. "You spend way too much time working. Between the marketing job and the catering business, when are you going to get out and find yourself a hot, sexy man? Hell, you're a gorgeous woman. I know someone at one of those parties had to ask you out on a date."

*You would fall out of that chair baby sister if I told you who wanted a date with me,* Cherise thought. "I don't cater dinner parties to find a man," she stated. "I enjoy cooking and having people take pleasure in a good meal."

"I'm just saying you can cook somewhere beside the kitchen," Traci complained. "Maybe if you spiced up your sex life, you could heat up other areas of your life."

Cherise couldn't believe her sister was giving her advice about sex. "Shouldn't you go check on Carter?"

Traci glared at her before she got up from the table and left the room. Cherise chuckled as she heard her sister mumble something under her breath. Ever since her baby sister got married, she has been trying so hard to find a man for her. Traci didn't understand at this time in her life she was too busy for a man. Plus, there wasn't a man out there she wanted a relationship with.

*Lee…Lee…Hmm…Aren't you forgetting about your handsome brother-in-law?* Her subconscious screamed at her, making her remember the elevator kiss. How much longer could she keep shoving Lee away from her? Forever, if she could just keep her mind and body on the same page. Lee couldn't ever be more to her than her overbearing brother-in-law. She wasn't going to make the same mistake twice in one lifetime.

Lee enjoyed flirting with her because he knew how much she hated it. It wouldn't ever amount to more than a few stolen kisses or touches here and there. Out of all the times he had kissed her in the past, none of them had been around other people. Each and every one of them occurred away from people. How could she believe anything that came out of his mouth when he couldn't come on to her around anyone else?

"Cherise, why are you mumbling about Lee?"

She glanced up to find Traci watching her from the kitchen doorway with a bewildered look on her face. "Oh, I was thinking out loud," Cherise lied.

"Why would you thinking about Lee? You hate him," Traci said, retaking her seat at the table.

"I don't hate him," she said correcting her sister. "I just feel he's a little too egotistical." Cherise prayed that Traci believed her story about Lee. It wouldn't do her any good if her sister found out about their stolen kisses. She would shove them together without a second thought.

"Lee uses his arrogance as a barrier. I think he's a very lonely man. He's about as bad as you when it comes to dating. I think Zack said that he went out with Amanda last night."

Cherise shoved down the jealously working its way through her body. "I thought they had broken up after the party I catered for her," she exclaimed, hating that she wanted to know more about Lee's date.

"That's what I thought, too, but the way Zack was talking, Lee might be trying to give Amanda another chance. Zack believes that Lee is getting tired of being alone."

"Amanda seems like the perfect accessory to Lee's good looks. They are a striking couple together," she sighed.

"I guess you're right," Traci agreed with her, making her feel even worse. "Hey, how about we stop talking about the Drace men and eat?"

After hearing about how Amanda was back in Lee's life, Cherise didn't have much of an appetite, but she couldn't let Traci know that. "We better eat before that husband of yours comes home or we won't get anything," Cherise laughed, trying to block out the images of Lee with Amanda.

\* \* \* \*

Lee held the three manila envelopes in his hand as he kicked the door closed with the heel of his shoe. As he walked back to his study, he flipped through the envelopes and wondered how well the three candidates did on the accounts he suggested to Justin. To make it a fair competition, he had the packages labeled 1, 2, and 3. He didn't want to judge on anything but the quality of the work.

He wanted something fresh and new to work on with the winner, plus he wanted some time away from the office. Brad was coming in so much more now since Alicia got different hours at work. He still wasn't fond of his youngest brother's feelings for the reporter. She kept using Brad to help her out with different projects, even though they weren't a couple. Brad said he didn't mind the friendship aspects first and he knew his brother was lying to him, but he wasn't going to say a word. He had enough problems trying to get some alone time with Cherise.

She had dogged him and the last three Drace family dinners and he was growing tired of it. If only he could find a way for the two of them to spend some quality time together, he could make her admit she wanted him as much as he desired her.

Inside his office, Lee sat down in the leather couch and tossed the envelopes on the table. He had lost count how many times he thought about kidnapping Cherise and bringing her in this room. He wanted to strip one of those sexy wraparound dresses from her curvaceous body and make love to her on this couch. Hell, he was getting fed up with self gratification when he knew Cherise would be a willingly partner.

Shit, the only thing that he wanted was an opening and he could take care of the rest. He didn't want to believe she was still holding the antique buy out against him. She had forgiven Zack months ago, so why was he any different? Lee hated how much he couldn't stop thinking about Cherise and what it would feel like to thrust in and out of that wonderful body of hers.

Oh, the first time they made love it was going to be slow and sweet. He would make it last until her perfectly manicured nails scratched at his back. She would scream his name as the first orgasms hit her. He had to pay her back from all the nights he woke up in bed with his hand wrapped around his hard cock.

Hell, she better hope that he didn't go through the entire box of condoms in one night with her. Because the way his body was hurting, it was going to be an all night event for the both of them. Lee felt his body hardening and pressing against the front of his jeans from just thinking about the different ways he wanted to take Cherise. Running his fingers through his hair, he jumped up from the couch and paced around the room. He needed to get himself under control or Cherise was going to be in a lot of trouble the next time he saw her.

The last couple of times it stopped at a few kisses, maybe some heavy petting, but next time he might have to sample those wonderful large nipples of hers. He caught a peek of them when she bent over to check a tray at the party Cherise catered for Amanda. He almost made a grab for her then, but a waiter came up and asked her a question. Next time, Cherise wasn't going to be so lucky.

Coming back over to the couch, Lee sat back down and picked up the first package again. He wanted to concentrate on this because he only had twenty hours to make a decision for Justin, but all he could think about was his stubborn sister-in-law. She hated him so much that she made the rest of the family not even tell him where her new job was at. Every time he asked, Zack would shake his head and say that he didn't know.

After this project was over with Crane Enterprises, he was going to Cherise's house and make her admit there was something sexual between them that should be explored to the fullest. The whole package of Cherise Roberts stroked a low burning blaze in the pit of his stomach. He wanted her to make it a full-blown inferno.

Lee finally shoved Cherise to the back of his mind and read over all the proposals for the ideas that he gave to Justin. After three long hours, he tossed the other two ideas on the table in front of him and held the winning idea in his hand. He loved everything about it from the way the outline was set up, to all the goals the person wanted to achieve.

He couldn't wait until he found out who the genius was that came up with these hot marketing prospects. Grabbing the two losing proposals and shoved them into the white envelope with the words 'rejected' written across the front in red ink. Picking up the winning proposal, he shoved it back into the manila envelope on the couch.

Now he wished that he had agreed to Justin's suggestion that he should meet the three candidates first. He didn't want to get stuck with some young asshole that couldn't or wouldn't take direction from him. Snatching his cell phone up off the table, he punched in the number for the all night delivery service and gave the guy the information that he wanted.

After he ended the call with the carrier, Lee tapped the phone on his denim-clad thigh and ran the forbidden thought through his head. He thought about it a couple of times before he worked up enough nerve to do it. He punched one on his speed dial before he could talk himself out of it. The phone rung three times before a sleepy soft female voice answered.

"Hello?"

"Are you in bed?" he whispered.

"Who is this?"

"Better yet, are you naked in bed touching that sweet body of yours?" Just the thought of Cherise pleasuring herself made his cock swell and twitch in his jeans.

"Lee, I know this better not be you," Cherise snapped, but he heard the catch in her voice. Did his words make her hot?

"Who else would be calling you wanting phone sex at twelve o'clock at night?" he questioned.

"Wouldn't you like to know?" Cherise taunted before her phone slammed down in his ear.

The pesky sound rung in his ear a few seconds before he snapped his phone closed and flung it down on the couch. "Fuck," Lee cursed, running his hand along the back of his neck. He never remembered a woman keeping him in knots like Cherise did. "That woman knows she's driving me crazy and she's enjoying it." When the time came, he was going to have a good time taming that sharp tongue of Cherise's.

Pulling his shirt over his head, Lee stormed out of the study for his bedroom. Tonight a cold shower wasn't going to help that ache his phone call caused. He needed some stroking to make him forget the sound of Cherise's sexy whisper on the phone. Hopefully, the Jasmine scented massage oil he brought yesterday would help him. It was the same scent his delectable sister-in-law was wearing the last time she came to dinner last month.

# *Chapter Four*

Cherise sat in the boardroom across from Missy, ignoring her non-stop talking to David, and wondered had a decision already been made about the marketing proposals. She had worked hard on that pitch and felt she deserved the job as much as or more than Missy, who she secretly thought just landed the job because of her resemblance to Jessica Simpson.

"Hey, you look like your mind is about twenty miles away," David teased breaking into her thoughts. "What's going on in that gorgeous head of yours?" he teased. "Man problems?"

At the mention of man problems, Lee's twinkling eyes and killer smiled popped up in her head. Yeah, man problem with her persistent brother-in-law. She had the hardest time falling back to sleep last night after his phone call. What in the hell had gotten into him to make him call her like that?

"No…not man problems," she answered, keeping her private thoughts to herself. "I was just thinking about who the freelancer is going to be."

"David, you know Cherise doesn't have any one in her life," Missy smirked. "Women like her stay at home and bake cookies for the neighborhood kids."

*You little bitch.* Cherise's mind screamed. "What makes you say something like that?" she questioned with more than a little heat to her voice. She was getting tired of Missy's jabs at her. Job or no job, if Missy kept it up, she was going to put the chick in her place. *Right under the bottom of my three-inch heels.*

Tilting her head to the side, Missy arched an eyebrow at her and ran her fingers through her hair. "You just don't seem like the type to get a man all hot and bothered. You're way too aloof for that."

"Aloof? Is that a younger way of saying I'm old?" Cherise hissed through clenched teeth.

"Well…" Missy drawled, smirking at her.

She started to tell the girl what she thought of her when David cleared his throat. "Cherise, don't let Missy drag you down that juvenile road. You're better than her and, by the way, I see Mr. Crane coming down the hall."

Glancing over her shoulder, she looked out the conference room windows and spotted Mr. Crane coming towards them. Great…now she had to calm down before he got here, so a pissed off look wouldn't be on her face.

She took several deep breaths and rotated her shoulders to ease some of the tension from them. Slowly, all the anger she felt toward Missy slid from her body. It wouldn't do her any good to lose her temper about Missy. Brushing her hand away from her cheek, she made eye contact with Missy then David, and then waited for Mr. Crane to arrive.

* * * *

"Good morning, ladies and gentleman," Justin said, coming into the conference room and closing the door behind him. Making his way over to a chair, he took a seat and tossed a file on the table next to her arm.

"Good morning, sir," Cherise replied, glancing up at her boss. Missy and David quickly said their greetings after her.

"It's good to see everyone here bright and early this morning," Justin smiled. "I sent the proposals over to the freelancer last night and I got them back within a few hours. He loved all of them, but only one stood out to him."

Cherise slid her hands into her lap and crossed her fingers. If she got this project and the colossal bonus that came with it, she could open a catering business. Instead of cooking all the meals out of her kitchen and she truly needed the extra space. Biting her lip, she studied Mr. Crane from the corner of her eye, but his expression wasn't giving anything away.

*Please God, let me get this.*

"All right, I'm not going to drag this out anymore than it should be. Congratulations, Ms. Roberts, your marketing plan was picked. Sorry I had to be the one to tell you, but the freelancer got caught up at work. He'll be here in about an hour."

Cherise couldn't keep the smile, that spread from ear to ear, off her face. Mr. Crane didn't know how much this extra money was going to come in handy for her. "Thank you, sir," Cherise replied, noticing the evil eye that Missy was giving her. She was counting the seconds until Missy's mouth screeched something it shouldn't.

"I don't think it's fair that Cherise got chosen," Missy pouted. "She has been here less time than any of us."

Cherise watched Mr. Crane pin Missy with a hard stare until she squirmed in her seat. "Ms. Payne, I already have a long day ahead of me. Please don't make it longer." He brought his eyes back over to her and smiled. "Congratulations again, Ms. Roberts. When your new partner gets here, I'll send him back to your office," Justin said, getting up from his seat and then he left the room.

"Congrats, Cherise, you deserve it," David grinned. He stood up and pulled Missy up with him. "I know you'll do a wonderful job. Come on, Missy, let's go. I think Cherise might like some time alone."

"Fine," Missy sighed as she glared at her. "But I still think the wrong person won," she complained as David tugged her out of the room behind him, away from her.

Shaking her head, Cherise sat at the conference room table for ten more minutes allowing the news to sink into her head. *I got the job!* She couldn't wait until she got home to call Traci. This was just the thing she needed to get her mind off Lee and her other problems. Who needed an active sex life when she would be able to earn the extra money for her new business?

Cherise picked the file up off the desk and left the room feeling a lot happier than she had in months or maybe years. Her luck was finally beginning to turn around for her. After she aced this assignment with the freelancer, maybe Mr. Crane would give her some of the more exclusive marketing accounts. Turning the corner, she walked the last few steps to her office and strolled through the open door.

She didn't have the biggest room at the firm, but it had a window that overlooked a park for which she was grateful. Anytime she wanted to be alone, all she had to do was shut the door and block out the noise from the office.

Sighing, she ran her hand through her hair. Cherise went over to her desk and sat down wondering about who she was going to get to work with. Maybe it would be some hot guy that would fall instantly in love with her.

*Now you're too old to be having daydreams like that.* But, it was a good fantasy while it lasted those few seconds. How would it feel to have a man who loved her, flaws and all? One that wouldn't mind she was a strong, confident woman that didn't need to be directed? Maybe if she closed her eyes and prayed, he would walk through that door. She slowly closed her eyes and wished for the man that she was meant to be with.

"Hey, Sunshine….you don't have to pray to see me. I'm right here," a masculine voice rumbled as her office door slammed shut.

* * * *

Cherise's eyes popped open at the same time an unladylike curse left her month. Swinging her head around towards the door, she connected eyes with Lee. He was leaning back against the door, looking hotter than any man had the right to. She tried calm down her beating heart. She tried to block out how handsome Lee looked in his dark blue suit with a green tie for a splash of color. Lee was always wearing some sort of colored tie with his darker suit. He must have known how much it turned her on and did it on purpose.

"How did you know where I worked?" she asked, staring at how the suit jacket stretched across the muscles in his arms. "I made Zack promise not to tell you." She knew now that her brother-in-law couldn't keep a secret.

"Zack didn't tell me where you worked. He always kept a tight lip about it," Lee said, walking away from the door towards her.

She wanted to move out of the chair, but she was frozen to the spot waiting to see what Lee was going to do. "I don't believe you. He had to have told you; if not, one of your other brothers did," Cherise uttered, standing up.

Closing the space between them in two long strides, Lee placed his hands on her shoulder and forced her back down into the seat. "No…you can't leave yet. I have to tell you something."

"I'm sure there's nothing that you have to say I want to hear, Lee," she exclaimed, placing her hand on his chest to shove him back. A tingling sensation shot through her hands on all the way through her body at the innocent touch. Dropping her hand quickly, she leaned her back away from Lee. *I wonder, did he feel the same thing?*

51

"Yes...I felt the spark between us, too," Lee whispered. Picking up her hand off the chair, he kissed the back of it and then winked at her.

Jerking her hand away from him, Cherise placed in the middle of her lap and frowned at Lee. "Why are you here?" she asked, secretly breathing in the powerful smell of his cologne.

Lee eased away from her and rested his back at the side of her desk. A look of pure amusement passed over his handsome features as he stared down at her. "You really haven't figured it out yet, have you?"

She shook her head and waited.

"Congrats.....you're looking at your new partner."

"You're lying," she whispered, jumping up out of her chair. Cherise brushed past Lee and started to pace around her office. "Fate wouldn't be this cruel to me. I can't be working with you," she muttered under her breath, not knowing how much her words cut the man at her desk.

"What's so wrong with working with me?" Lee asked, falling down into her chair. "I think we'll make a great team. We're both intelligent, well-focused people that know how to get a job done."

Cherise couldn't even believe that Lee was considering the idea of them working side by side on this project. She stopped her pacing and stared at Lee sitting in her seat and a smile slowly spread across her face. "What am I worried about is that Mr. Crane won't let it stand once he finds out we are related."

"He already knows and doesn't have a problem with it," Lee tossed out knocking the wind out of her sails. "Don't you think he had to tell me who won when I got here? I had to come and introduce myself to you, didn't I?"

"Shit!"

"Now, that isn't the kind of language a woman like yourself should be using," Lee teased as he propped his

Italian leather shoes on her desk. "I rather hear other words come from that sexy mouth of yours."

Storming back over to her desk, Cherise knocked Lee's shoes off her desk. "Okay, you want to hear something else? How about get out of my office?" she snapped.

Lee didn't flinch at her outburst. He only flashed a grin and shook his dark head. "No. I was thinking of something more like 'Kiss me, Lee'."

Cherise rolled her eyes and then muttered. "Kiss me, Lee. Why would I...?" Her next words were cut off as Lee reached out and jerked her down into his hard thighs.

"I thought you would never ask," he growled, before his lips completely covered hers.

# Chapter Five

*Hot sex on a cold winter night.*

That's the thought that was racing through Cherise's mind as Lee's tongue slipped its way inside of her mouth. She tried to think of a million reasons to push him away, but she couldn't. Instead, she got lost in the moment and wrapped her arms around his neck. Purring in the back of throat, she let herself get lost in the kiss.

"Damn, Sunshine, you taste so good," Lee whispered as his teeth nibbled at her bottom lip. "I could get lost in your mouth for the rest of the day."

Closing her eyes, Cherise slowly counted to ten and then eased her body away from Lee. He shouldn't have the power to be able to do this to her. They were bitter enemies. He took her beloved antique shop away from her. What was she doing in his lap playing tonsil hockey?

"Well, I don't have the rest of the day to sit here while you take advantage of me. I need to get back to work," Cherise complained as she quickly climbed out of Lee's lap. She tried to ignore the hard erection that brushed her thigh.

"You're such a workaholic. Do you always approach all of your relationships with such passion?" Lee chuckled behind her. The chair squeaked under his weight as he moved around in it.

"When I care about something, I give it all that I have," she answered, trying to ignore the double meaning of his comment.

"So, I can expect the same passion when we get involved with each other?"

"First, I hate you and secondly, we'll never have a relationship beyond our family ties."

"My little tigress is showing her claws today. I should be hurt by your words, yet they only make me hotter. I can't wait until I finally win you over. It's going to be the greatest accomplishment in my life."

Cherise spun around and stared at Lee. "Why aren't you bothering your girlfriend, Amanda? I'm sure she'll enjoy your company."

"Jealousy doesn't become you, but I'm flattered you're envious. However, Amanda isn't my girlfriend. I only want one woman and it's you. Now, how about you stop trying to pick a fight with me?"

"I'm not trying to pick a fight with you," she pouted, hating how well Lee could read her.

"Yes, you are."

"Lee, why are you still here? Don't you have your own business to run? Can't you just leave and let me enjoy the rest of my day?"

A rakish grin covered Lee's sensual mouth as he got up from the chair and made his way over to her. "Nope, we have to go over your marketing package. Which, by the way, I was very impressed with."

"I still think it is a conflict of interest, the two of us working together," she answered, taking a step back. Cherise knew she couldn't let Lee touch her again or things would get out of hand.

"Why because you want to see me naked in your bed or is it because you can't keep your hands off me," Lee smirked.

"You're way too cocky for you own good," she sighed trying not to laugh at Lee. He was something else, but he did have one hell of a sense of humor.

"Okay. I'll leave you alone, but this conversation isn't over. However, I do have something to ask you."

"Lord. What is it?"

"Traci wanted to know if you would watch Carter tonight for her. Zack wants to take her out for a romantic date."

"Tonight?"

"Yeah, tonight," Lee answered.

"I can't," Cherise sighed. "I've got other plans."

"With whom?" Lee demanded. "Are they with a man?"

Cherise opened her mouth to answer Lee's questions, but David came through the door stopping her. "Oh, I'm sorry. I didn't know you had someone in here with you."

She couldn't help but smile at the wide-eyed look on her co-worker's face. She seldom had visitors at work and if any one did come by, it was usually Traci with the baby.

"Don't worry about it. What can I do for you?"

"I just wanted to make sure that you were still coming over tonight," David asked.

"Yes. I'll be there around six o'clock. Did you remember to buy everything that I told you?"

"I forgot the chocolate syrup."

"Don't worry about it. I have some at home. I'll bring it with me," she replied, very aware of how tense Lee was becoming.

"Great," David grinned. "I'll see you later." He gave Lee another quick glance and then hurried out the door shutting it behind him.

"Why in the hell do you need to bring chocolate syrup to his house?" Lee's deep voice thundered beside her.

"That's none of your business, and I think it's time for you to leave." Going over to the door, she opened it up and waited for her brother-in-law to leave.

"Cherise, I want an answer," Lee demanded, storming across the room. "Are you dating him?"

"Lee, you really need to leave. I've work to do."

"I'm going but you can't avoid me much longer since we're going to be partners for a while." Before she could move, Lee planted a quick kiss on her mouth and then strolled out the door like he owned the world.

"God, I truly do hate him," Cherise sighed as her lips still tingled from Lee's kiss.

# *Chapter Six*

"Are you sure that you're up to watching him?" Traci asked, placing the baby in his arms. Carter grinned at him and then reached for his necklace.

"Traci, I helped raise my brothers," Lee laughed. "I think I can handle watching my nephew for a few hours."

"I hate it that Cherise has a date tonight and couldn't watch him. Carter loves her so much."

"Cherise isn't on a date," Lee snapped so loud that it made Carter whimper in his arms.

"Lee, you need to calm down and stop scaring my son," Zack said. "Or you can leave and we'll stay home."

Lee felt bad. He didn't want his brother or Traci to miss out on their date because of his bad mood. Plus, he never got to spend any quality time with his nephew, so that's why he volunteered to take Cherise's place.

"Guys, I'm sorry. I shouldn't have yelled. Carter is going to be fine with me. I'm going to play with him and tell him all about the wonders of the world. He'll be in good hands."

Traci glanced at him and then back at Zack. "Come on, honey. I know Lee won't let anything happen to Carter. I really want this date tonight."

"Zack, do you honestly want to disappointment your gorgeous wife?"

"I guess not," Zack answered, going towards the closet. He opened it up and pulled out a black coat for Traci.

58

Lee watched while his brother helped Traci put on the coat and then as he planted a kiss on the back of his wife's neck. Traci and Cherise were so different. Cherise would rather freeze to death than let him help her put on a coat. God…he loved how obstinate his sister-in-law was, but he was going to break her down, sooner or later.

"I want the two of you to have fun," he said, switching Carter over to his left side as his nephew started to play with a button on his shirt. "I have all of this taken care of. Carter and I are going to have a wonderful time."

"Lee, are you sure?" Traci asked, opening the front door. "He looks all sweet and loving, but my little man can be a handful when he wants to."

"I think I can handle an eight-month-old baby," Lee laughed, kissing his nephew on the cheek.

He ignored Zack's chuckle as he followed Traci out the door. "Sure you can, but if you run into any trouble, Cherise's cell phone is on the refrigerator. Don't be too proud to call her. However, do not call her unless it's important."

Walking to the door, he glared at Zack as he followed Traci to the car and Lee stood there until they got into the vehicle and drove off. "Carter, I don't know what is wrong with your parents. They don't think I can handle a baby, but we're going to show them, aren't we?" he asked, closing the door.

* * * *

Cherise stood to the side and tried not to laugh as David tried to add the little drop of chocolate to the center of the muffin. His hands were shaking so bad because he wanted to impress his wife with these new treats he was trying to learn how to make for her.

"David, calm down. It isn't that hard to do. Just take your time and everything will be okay," she laughed.

"Cherise, Mary loved these when you brought them over last month and I want to learn how to make them for her. Yours looked so perfect with the different chocolate, vanilla and strawberry in the middle. If I can't get the chocolate down, how do you expect me to be able to do the other ones?" he complained, sitting the pastry bag down on the counter. "I give up. I can do it."

Shaking her head, Cherise moved closer to David. Picking up the pastry bag, she added the little drops of chocolate. "You're trying too hard. It's not difficult to do at all."

"Sure, you can say that because you just zipped through it. I don't have the same talent as you do," David sighed. He picked up a treat and took a bite.

"God, you have magic hands when it comes to food. Why do you waste your time at the marketing firm? You should open up your own catering business and sell these things for twenty dollars each. I know you would be a success."

"First, I love working at the firm despite the fact that Missy does get on my last nerve. I think she's trying to make me snap at her so I can lose my job."

"Missy does seem to hate you for some reason. I think she might be jealous."

"Missy isn't jealous of me. She's just a plain bitch."

David finished off his treat and reached for another one. "You're right. She is. However, she's very smart and knows how to push your buttons. I heard her talking about that guy in your office today. Who was he anyway?"

"What did she say about Lee?" Cherise asked, trying not to sound jealous, but she was. Missy was the type who would flirt with Lee in a heartbeat.

"Lee…as in the crazy brother-in-law that doesn't know how to leave you alone?" David asked. "I've heard you talk about him but never seen him until now. He's a big something, isn't he? How tall is he?"

"I think he's around six feet six inches and he loves to use his height to intimidate me. I hate him with a passion," Cherise lied.

"Sure you do," David laughed. "That's why you got this look on your face when I mentioned Missy was looking at him."

"What look? I didn't get a look."

"Yes, you did. You looked like your world had ended. You're in love with him, aren't you?"

Cherise picked up the pastry bag and shoved it into her cooking purse on the counter. She couldn't admit how she was starting to feel about Lee to anyone. It was still her secret. "You don't know what you're talking about."

"Okay…if you say so," David laughed, then handed her the rest of her cooking supplies. "I guess you're going to leave now."

"Yep, I want to be gone before Mary gets home so you can show her the treats that you made."

"Technically, I didn't make them." David took the sweets out of the pan and placed them on a plate by the sink. "I don't want to lie to her."

"You did make them. All I did was add the chocolate. Maybe you can teach Mary how to do them and then have fun working with the chocolate later."

David blushed under his olive complexion and quickly handed her bag to her. "I think you need to leave. I'm not used to this fun side of you."

"Hey, I know how to kick back and have fun when I have to," she said, taking the bag from David. She gave him a quick hug and then headed to the door. "I'll see you tomorrow at work."

"Okay and don't forget to take your nerve pill before you come. You know Missy will be gunning for you."

Opening the door, Cherise waved goodbye to David and then closed it behind her. She didn't have time to deal with David and his crazy sense of humor, not tonight away. Cherise was on her way to her car when cell phone started to ring. Pausing in the middle of the driveway, she dug it out of her purse and answered it.

"Yes."

"Can you come over to Traci's? There's something wrong with Carter," Lee said in her ear.

"What's wrong with the baby?" she asked, as she rushed to her car and got inside.

"I don't know. Can you please hurry?" Lee exclaimed, making her heart drop to the pit of her stomach. "The front door will be unlocked, so come on in."

"I'm on my way. I'm not that far away. I should be there in twenty minutes." Cherise ended the call and tossed her phone back into her purse. Starting the car, she backed out of David's driveway and then headed in the direction of her sister's house.

Cherise made record time getting there. She got out of the car and raced up the steps to her sister's house. She didn't even bother to knock as she opened the door and went on in.

She hurried up to Lee who was walking back and forth in the living room with a crying Carter in his arms. "What happened? Why is he crying?"

Lee stopped in his tracks and looked down at her. She blocked out how good he looked in his jeans and white Polo shirt. She was here to see about her nephew and not drool over his sexy uncle.

"I don't know. He started crying about an hour ago and I can't get him to stop," Lee sighed, looking flustered and upset.

"Give him to me," she said reaching for the crying baby. Lee placed Carter in her arms and then took a seat on the couch behind him. "I wish you luck, because nothing I did made him stop."

Pressing the crying child against her shoulder, Cherise started to rub his back slowly and rock him as she walked around the living room. "It's okay, Carter. Your Auntie Cherise is here now."

The tears kept pouring as Carter snuggled closer to her and grabbed some of her shirt inside his small fist. "Don't cry, sweetheart," she whispered against the baby's ear. She never stopped rubbing his back and trying to soothe whatever was wrong with her precious nephew. After a few minutes, the crying stopped and Carter's breathing slowed down.

Easing over to the couch, Cherise sat down next to Lee but she didn't stop patting Carter's back. "I can't believe you didn't call me sooner," she said, tossing the man of her torment a look. She was trying her best not to notice how good he smelled.

"I didn't want to bother you on your date with David. How did it go by the way?" Lee asked, stretching his arm out on the back of the couch. His body heat surrounded them making her forget all about her cooking lesson with David earlier.

"It went fine. He had a little problem putting the chocolate in the hole, but I think with some practice he'll get a lot better."

"Why in the hell was he putting chocolate in your hole?" Lee roared, making Carter whimper in his sleep.

"Listen, don't you yell and wake up the baby," Cherise hissed under her breath.

"How do you expect me not to yell when you tell me another man was putting chocolate on you?"

*Where does he come up with this stuff?*

"David wasn't placing chocolate on my body. I was teaching him how to fix a dessert for his wife."

"Oh, well, what do you expect me to think when you tell me stuff like that?" Lee accused, looking at her. "I get jealous when I think about other men touching what is mine."

Cherise's heart jumped in chest at Lee's possessive words, but she shoved it back down. It would never work out between the two of them. She loved having her freedom and Lee wanted to dominate her way too much. They would never find a common ground.

"I'm not yours."

"Sunshine, you've been mine since the moment I laid eyes on you in the antique shop," Lee whispered by her ear. "Now all I have to do is make you believe it."

She would love to be able to think that the words coming out of Lee's mouth was the truth, but she knew better. Past experiences had taught her that.

"I'm going to love winning you over. Maybe we'll get lucky enough to have a baby as beautiful as Carter."

Cherise's body warmed at the thought of a baby. She loved her nephew so much, but Lee was just teasing about having a baby with her. He would end up with someone like Amanda. He was just toying with her.

"You'll probably have a very cute baby, but it won't be with me. I know you aren't serious about me."

"Who hurt you?" Lee asked out of the blue, shocking the hell out of Cherise. "You didn't get like this on your own. Did a man hurt you?"

Almond-colored eyes and a sly smile flashed in front of Cherise's face before she blinked it away. No, she wasn't going to think about Chad. He was part of her past and he would stay there.

"I need to put Carter in his crib and then I have to go." She got up from the couch and hurried past Lee before he could stop her.

Lee watched Cherise leave and fought back the urge to follow her. Something in her past was keeping her from believing that he honestly wanted a relationship with her. He would find out what demons she was hiding and get rid of them. He couldn't fight a ghost unless he knew what it was, but he wasn't giving up. He wanted Cherise in his life. She was meant to be his wife and it would happen sooner rather than later.

# *Chapter Seven*

"Please tell me you're kidding," Cherise asked, wrapping the bathrobe tighter around her body. "This can't be happening to me." She had gotten up this morning to running water, and about five minutes into her shower it stopped. Now a plumber was here telling her that most of her pipes needed to be replaced.

"Ma'am, I wish that I was," he replied, "but I'm not. Your pipes are gone and they need to be replaced as soon as possible."

"Isn't there a way I can at least stay here while you're fixing them?" She didn't want to think about the money she would have to spend on a hotel.

"I think it would be best if you didn't try to use any water while we replace these pipes. We aren't positive how good the other ones are until we look at them."

Cherise stood in the middle of her yard and looked at the areas the plumber said would have to be dug up. This was going to cost her a small fortune, but she loved her old house and didn't have it in her heart to sell it.

"I guess you can go ahead and do it," she sighed, already hating the check she was going to have to write.

"Okay…let me take a better look at everything and I can give you an estimate." The plumber patted her on the shoulder and then walked around the side of her house.

"Why does this kind of stuff always happen to me?" Cherise mumbled under her breath.

"Do you mind telling me why you're outside wrapped in a barely-there robe? I don't want to fight off your male neighbors for looking at your gorgeous body," Lee's voice demanded behind her. "I've been at work waiting for you for almost an hour. What in the hell is going on?"

*Great*, she thought. Lee was all that she needed this morning.

"Didn't you get my message? I told them that I might be a little late this morning," she said, looking at her house and not at the temping man behind her. Her dreams were filled of him doing wicked things to her body and she hated it when the alarm clock woke her up this morning.

"I consider being late maybe fifteen to thirty minutes not a whole damn hour. So, I got concerned and came to check on you, but I find you outside in your bathrobe showing off your amazing breasts to the world. Now, tell me what in the hell is going on?"

Spinning around, Cherise gasped at the sight of Lee in a dark pinstriped suit and a dark green shirt with no tie. He totally looked amazing without a tie! God, why did her brother-in-law have to be so damn fine!

"I'm having trouble with my pipes."

"You're pipes look pretty good to me, Sunshine," Lee whispered as he reached out and slipped his hand inside of her robe. Cupping one of her breasts, he ran his thumb over the nipple. It hardened instantly under his touch.

"Lee, what are you doing?" Cherise hissed, trying to remove Lee's hand from her body. He was making her hot and this couldn't be happening, not outside in her front yard.

"Shhh…come closer," he whispered as he tugged her body against his. "I want to touch you." Lee's hand eased down her body and brushed against her moist curls. "You're already wet. Have you been thinking about me?" Two thick fingers moved down a little further and dipped into her body.

"Oh, shit," Cherise whimpered as Lee's fingers worked in and out of her. His free hand held her butt and gave it a squeeze. She knew she should stop him, but it was so hard to think straight when Lee was this close to her.

"I love a woman that can handle me," he growled by her ear. "I'm a big man and I need someone that can take me loving them."

Wow! She bet that Lee could love her right, but she couldn't get seduced by him. They had to work together and more than that, he was family now. If anything went wrong, it would put a strain on her sister's marriage to Zack. She couldn't do that to Traci.

"Lee, please stop," she whimpered, tugging Lee's hand from her body. "We have to stop. This isn't right. We're family." She took a step back from Lee so she wouldn't be tempted to kiss him.

"We're only family through marriage. So, I can enjoy that wonderful luscious body of yours anyway I want. All you have to do is give me the green light and I'll take you right here in the middle of the yard. I don't give a damn who sees us."

Cherise pulled her robe tighter around her body and tried to not think about how good Lee would feel inside of her. "Stop talking like that. It isn't right. You're my brother-in-law. We can't have a relationship with each other. You have to date someone else and so will I."

"The hell you will date another man around me. I'll make sure he understands who you belong to. You're mine and I don't share."

"Lee, I'm not dating anyone. I don't have time for a man in my life. I'm busy with work and my catering business, so why don't we just leave it alone?"

"Tell me the guy who did such a number on you that you think the only pleasure you can have in life is work. You're a beautiful woman that deserves a good man."

Where was the cocky Lee from a few seconds ago? This understanding Lee was too much for her to handle.

She would rather fight with him. "Lee, why don't you go back to work and I'll be there as soon as I can." She shivered as the cold air hit her. It was early October and she didn't know why she was outside in the damn cold.

"Here, take my jacket." Lee held out his suit jacket while she slipped it on. It wrapped completely around her. Most guys' jackets didn't do that. Lee was truly a huge guy and there wasn't an ounce of fat on his entire body. It was solid muscle. "Now are you going to tell me why you're out here?"

The warm scent of his cologne filled her nose and the warmth from the jacket heated up her body. "My water pipes busted this morning while I was in the shower. The plumber is checking on them so he can give me an estimate of how much it will cost. So, now I have to stay at a hotel until they get fixed."

"You aren't going to stay at a hotel," Lee said, wrapping his arms around her waist. "I know the perfect place for you to stay."

"Is that right, Mister Know-It-All? Where do you think I'm going to stay? I'm not going to ask Traci if I can crash at her house. I know Zack likes me better now, but he still wants some private time with his wife."

"Of course. You aren't going to stay with them. Sunshine, you going to stay with me," Lee said in her ear. "I have a bed at my house that's screaming your name."

The shock of Lee's words almost made her pass out. There was no way in hell she would be staying under the same roof as him. "You're out of your mind. I can't stay under the same roof as you. We'll kill each other."

"With sex?" Lee asked at the same time the plumber came back around the house.

# *Chapter Eight*

"I can't believe you embarrassed me like that in front of that guy. Lord only knows what he thinks about me now. I have to deal with him while he works on my house," Cherise snapped, tossing the bill the plumber left her down on the table.

"Hey, I didn't know he'd be coming around the house at the same time I was talking about making love to you. So, are you up to the challenge?"

She was at her wit's end with Lee. He was driving her up the wall. Why couldn't he listen when she talked to him? "No, I'm not up to the challenge because we aren't ever going to sleep in the same bed. I'm staying at a hotel and that's final."

"Cherise, you aren't about to stay at any damn hotel. I have a huge house with more than enough rooms. You can pick which one you want to stay in, but you're going to stay with me and that's final," Lee snapped, daring her to argue.

"In case you haven't noticed, I'm a grown-ass woman and I don't take well to orders, Lee. I was beginning to like you as my brother-in-law. But if you keep up with the attitude, you'll go right back at the top of my hate list."

The heated look Lee flashed her way made her take a step back. Flashing a wicked grin, he advanced towards her until he had her back pressed against the wall. "Cherise, I know you're a woman. Your beautiful breasts make it hard for me not to," he whispered as he knocked his jacket off her shoulders.

Cupping her left breast in his hand, Lee ran his blunt nail across the tip. "Do you know how many times I dream about sucking on these as we make love?"

She grabbed Lee's wrist and shook her head. "Stop, we can't do this."

"Baby, we can do anything we want. I'm ready to learn the pleasure your beautiful body can give to me."

"It's not going to happen. You should just give it up," Cherise said, trying to believe the words she was saying to Lee. "You're just playing with me. You really don't want me."

"Do you think this is fake?" Removing her hand from his wrist, Lee placed it on the front of his slacks. The heat from his cock burned into her palm making moisture pool between her thighs.

"Shit…last week at dinner I almost came in my pants when you walked in wearing that red shirt and those tights-ass jeans. All I wanted to do was carry you upstairs and keep you in my bed."

"If I got you so hot and bothered, why did you leave the table so quickly after I got there?" She tried to move her hand, but Lee pressed it even closer.

"I had to go and take care of my problem. I swear my dick had never been that hard before. I was thinking of a way to get my brothers and Traci to leave."

Cherise knew she shouldn't let Lee talk to her like this, but she couldn't help it. It was turning her on and it had been such a long time since a man had done that for her. "You were gone a long time. I can't believe all that time you were pleasing yourself."

"Sunshine, anytime I get hard from thinking about you or seeing you, once isn't enough. I have to come again and again. I think about how good your warm hand will feel on me and it starts all over."

"So, the only thing you want from me is sex," she accused, softly jerking her hand from under his. "I was

71

right about you." Cherise tried to move around Lee's body, but he placed a hand above her head blocking her in with his powerful body.

"Move out of my way," she whispered, glancing way from his penetrating eyes. Memories of Chad had come back full force and she wasn't going down that road again. Lee really wasn't any different.

"Look at me," he demanded.

"No."

A few seconds ticked by as Lee stared at the side of her face and she waited for him to walk away like most men did when she got to be too much for them.

"I'm sorry," Lee whispered softly.

Shocked by the apology, Cherise's head spun around and she stared up at the man that was slowly trying to tear down the walls around her heart. "What?"

"I shouldn't have talked to you like that. I want more than just sex from you. I want a relationship with you. I've been attracted to you since that first moment I saw you in the antique shop. You're a complex woman and I like that about you. Can't you think about giving us a try?"

"I can't."

Disappointment clouded Lee's eyes and in a flash, it was gone. Cherise almost thought that she had missed it. "We can have a working relationship and be friends because we're family, but I can't agree to anything else."

"I understand," Lee answered stepping back from her. "But I still want you to move in with me. You're family, and I swear I won't make one move on you while you're there. I understand where I stand with you now."

Cherise felt like she was making the biggest mistake of her life. However, she knew that if she gave her heart to Lee and he broke it, she would never recover. "Okay, I'll pack up some stuff and move in later today."

"Great," Lee answered and then bent down picking his jacket up off the floor. "Take your time getting to work. I can start looking over your proposal again and come up with some ideas."

She stood still against the wall and watched as Lee redressed and a part of her wondered should she give him a chance. Maybe he wouldn't be critical of her like Chad had been, but she shoved the thought from her mind. Lee was a hundred times better looking and hotter than her ex-boyfriend. He wouldn't be any different.

"I'll see you later," Lee said and then walked past her and out the door without looking back.

"Don't you dare cry," Cherise whispered as she brushed a tear away from her cheek. "You did the right thing. Lee Drace is too much man and way too cocky for you."

# Chapter Nine

"Okay, what's going on with you and Lee?" her sister's voice asked behind her as she slid a tray of cookies into the oven. Lee's kitchen was three times the size of hers at home and she couldn't stop cooking and baking.

"What are you talking about?" Cherise set the timer and faced her sister. Traci looked too cute in her black jeans and pinstriped shirt. It was one of those rare days that her sister wasn't at the hospital working. Zack was pushing Traci to open her own practice after she graduated, but her sister wasn't going for it.

"Where's my Carter?" she asked, taking a seat at the table. Traci pulled out a chair and joined her.

"Zack took him to work with him and then he's taking him to the park. It's their guy day. I'm pretty sure that Carter is too young to realize it, but Zack loves it."

"Zack is really a good man. I'm glad that my opinion of him changed."

"Yeah, he likes you a lot better now, too. Zack doesn't think you're as bossy as you used to be."

"I was never bossy," Cherise frowned. "But I had the right to give my baby sister my opinion about the man in her life."

"Hmmm...speaking of men, where's Lee? Why didn't you stay with us instead of him? I thought the two of you hated each other. Is there something going on I should know about? Zack thinks the two of you are knocking the boots and Carter will have a cousin pretty soon."

Cherise couldn't believe that everyone was so interested in her non-relationship with Lee. She wasn't knocking anything with him, so there wasn't going to be another baby brought into the family.

"Tell Zack I'm not sleeping with his arrogant brother. My pipes at my house are busted and Lee invited me to stay here. I told him no, but you know how he is once his mind is made up. He won't take no for an answer."

"Are you sure that's the only reason he asked you to be his roommate?" Traci asked, arching an eyebrow. "I've seen how he looks at you. I think he wants to be the cream to your coffee."

"Cream to my coffee," she laughed. "Where in the hell do you come up with this stuff? Have you been talking to Brad? That craziness is something that he would say. By the way, how is he doing with getting a date with Alicia?"

"Brad hasn't been around us much lately. I think he pouting over the fact Alicia stopped her tennis lessons with him. She is playing with his emotions and I don't like it. If she doesn't want him, why doesn't she just let him go?"

"Have you thought that maybe she's scared? What if Brad is the one for her and she isn't ready to admit it?"

"Are we still talking about Alicia?"

"Yes," Cherise answered quickly. "Who else would I be talking about?'

Traci gave her a long look and then shrugged her shoulder. "I thought you might be talking about you and Lee. He really does like you, sis. Can't you give him a chance?"

"Traci, I can't do it. I won't have another Chad in my life. I'm doing well now. I have two jobs that I love and I'm losing a little weight."

"You're perfect the way you are." Traci reached across the table and grabbed her hand. "Don't get caught up in that weight loss thing again. You can work out with me anytime you want, but don't you dare start skipping meals again. I don't want you to end up in the hospital again. Chad was a first-class bastard and deserves a good beat down for what he did to you."

"He didn't do anything that I didn't allow, but he's out of my life now. Let's not talk about it anymore."

"Please don't tell me you think Lee will do the same thing Chad did. He is so much better than that. Do you know when you aren't around, he constantly asks about you?"

"Traci, I honestly don't have time for a man in my life," Cherise answered, hoping her sister would drop the subject.

"I'll let this go for now, but we aren't finished with this. Remember I told you that I was going to find you a man to fall in love with." Removing her hand, Traci stood up and looked down at her. "I have to go, but I'll call you later. I want you to bring me some of those cookies over to the house."

Smiling, Cherise stood up and hugged her sister. "I'll make sure to bring extra. I think you told me that Zack likes to carry them to work."

"Yep, he has a sweet tooth, but you couldn't tell by looking at his body."

"See…now I like Zack and all, but I'm not looking at his body," she laughed.

"Of course you aren't," Traci giggled ending the hug. "You're too busy checking out Lee." Winking at her, Traci left the kitchen and a few seconds later, she heard the front door closed.

# *Chapter Ten*

"How are things going with you and Cherise? Has she driven you up the wall yet? I still can't believe the two of you are still living under the same roof," Richard commented as he watched Dawn talk and laugh with a male customer. He hated when the men flirted with his fiancée, but he knew Dawn loved him.

"Things aren't going as I planned. Cherise avoids me at every turn and she knows what she's doing. How can I win her over if she's running from me? I love it when we fight with each other. It's such a turn on, but all she does now is agree with me and leave the room. Work isn't much better. She'll work side by side with me without taking any of my baits. I don't like how she is. I know that there is something is going on with her."

"Have you given any thought to that maybe Cherise isn't interested in you? I know that you're the great Lee Drace and all, but she might have another man in her life."

"Cherise is mine!" Lee growled. "I know without a doubt she wants me." How could he not after the way she responded to him outside in her yard? "I just have to find out the reason she's pushing me away and take care of it."

"Whatever you say," Richard said, looking at him then back over to Dawn.

"So, when are you going to marry her?"

"I keep asking her to pick a date and she tells me she isn't ready to get married. We have been together for months and I'm ready to make it official. I want men to know that she belongs to me."

"Is Hamilton still trying to steal her from you? I heard he offered her an enormous amount of money to come back to his restaurant."

"Hamilton knows that he better stay away from Dawn. That's another reason I want to get married. Dawn keeps having lunch with him and I hate it," Richard said. "She seems to ignore the fact the man has feelings for her."

"Do you think she'll cheat on you?"

"No....I know Dawn loves me and Hamilton is only her friend, but damn it, I want to get married and start having babies. However, Dawn is acting like she doesn't think I'm serious about it."

"I'm not the best person to ask about love life advice," he complained. "At least you have the woman you're in love with. Cherise is living under the same roof as me and I can't even touch her. Last night, she was working on a new recipe in the kitchen and she looked like she belonged in my home. I don't know how long I stood there watching her before I walked away."

"Lee, why are you doing this to yourself? Tell Cherise that you aren't going to stand for her blowing off what's happening between the two of you. Everyone sees the chemistry and it would be dumb not to act on it."

"I want to, but Cherise is so damn strong-willed. That little she-devil will do something just to piss me off so I'll leave her alone."

Richard's laughter made him look at his brother. "What are you laughing about?"

"I can't wait until I see the two of you married, because you two are going to light up the place. I swear I've never seen you work so hard to get a woman."

"I don't mind the fight because Cherise is the one for me," Lee sighed, "Now all I have to do is show her." He glanced down at his watch and groaned. "I better get back to work. Cherise is probably already there waiting for me and I think Justin is going to show some kind of video."

"How's the working relationship going between the two of you?"

"Fine, I guess. We don't argue at work, but she keeps her distance. You would never know that she won the competition to work with me. Her perfume drives me crazy everyday. It's so hard for me not to kiss her senseless every time she shows me something for our project."

"Are you going to give up on her? Is she really worth all of this time and trouble?"

Lee's eyes darkened as he stared at his brother. "Was Dawn worth all the trouble that you went through? Would you rather she stayed at Hamilton's restaurant instead of coming back to *D4* with you?"

His brother visibly tensed at the thought of the love of his life being with another man. "I would kill Hamilton if he thought about having a relationship with Dawn. She's the love of my life."

"Now, you know how I feel," he tossed back.

"Sorry...point taken. I wish you luck. Cherise is tough."

"I have the patience to wait for her." Lee slapped his brother on the back and then headed out the side entrance of the building. He wanted to make sure he got a seat beside her at the meeting. Her co-worker David spent way too much time with his woman. If he hadn't heard the guy talking about his wife with such love, he would think David had feelings for Cherise.

# *Chapter Eleven*

"I hope you enjoy your time with Lee because I'm going to take him from you. He isn't the type of man who'll want a woman like you."

Cherise closed her eyes and silently counted to ten as Missy's snippy voice sounded off behind her. What was this girl's problem with her? She was constantly in her face about something. Turning around from the window, she glanced at the girl who seemed to have a permanent scowl on her face.

"First, I'm not with Lee. He's working with me on the project and nothing more. Secondly, if you didn't know, he's my brother-in-law. Lee is family. So there will never be anything romantic between the two of us," Cherise lied, knowing just last night that she had a dream about Lee. It totally tossed him out of the family category. His fine ass was wearing her down and she couldn't let that happen.

Missy tilted her head to the side and eyed her like she could almost read her thoughts. "I don't believe you. There's no way you don't want a man as sexy as Lee. He doesn't care that he's part of your family. I've seen the way you look at him. You're lusting after him."

"Missy, leave Cherise alone," David chimed in as he walked into the room. "Every time I come around, you're in her face. Give it a rest and find another poor soul to bother for the next hour."

She gave David a wide smile as Missy flipped her hair over shoulder and stormed away acting like the child she was. "Thanks for saving me. I almost thought I was going to lose it with her."

David squeezed her shoulder and stood next to her. "Not a problem. I had to protect the best cook in the world, didn't I?"

Cherise knew something was up when David brought up her cooking. "What do you want me to fix for you?"

"I don't want a thing," he denied as his dark brown eyes connected with hers. "I was just being a good friend."

Laughing, she bumped David's shoulder with hers. "Come on and spill it. I know you want me to cook you something. Tell me what it is."

"Well…Mary's brother is coming to town and she was wondering if you could fix a small little dinner for four."

"Sure, I can. Just let me know when it is," Cherise answered. "I didn't know Mary had a brother."

"Yep and he's bringing his latest girlfriend with him. Mary doesn't think it the real thing, but she isn't about to say a word. Christopher is forty-two and still looking for his trophy wife."

"Hey, this woman that he's bringing might be the one."

"I seriously doubt that. He's can't see past a pretty face to find a good woman on the inside."

"I really hope that both of you are wrong. However, just let me know and I'll see what I can do for you."

Grinning, David leaned down and kissed her on the cheek. "You're a doll, and some man is going to be so lucky to have you as a wife."

Cherise wished that was true, but she wasn't going down that road again. Once she thought she loved a man enough to get married, but never again.

"Thanks for the kind words, but I'm never getting married," she sighed. "I'm going to stay single for the rest of my life."

"Really, does Lee know that?"

Her pulse raced at the sound of Lee's name. She tried to block him from her mind, but it was so hard. Lord, she hoped her pipes got fixed soon. Because coming downstairs in the morning, seeing him with his shirt hanging open, was driving her crazy.

He had the best-looking body she had ever seen on a man. Solid muscles were everywhere, not an ounce of fat anywhere on him. Even his damn belly button was turning her on and that was just plain old weird. She was acting like she was some damn virgin.

"Earth to Cherise….are you there?" David snapped his fingers in front of her face.

"I'm here and stop doing that," she snapped, swatting his fingers out of her face. She was amazed at how friendly she was with David because before Traci married Zack, she would have never look at David twice. She sure in hell wouldn't have thought about being his friend. So, Traci helped her overcome some stuff and she was proud of herself.

"Lee has nothing to do with my love life," she uttered.

"Don't lie to me. I've seen how he looks at you. He wants you and he isn't going to give up until he gets you. I know the look. It was the same one I had when I wanted Mary and I didn't stop until I got her."

"You're wrong," she denied.

"Sure I am," David chuckled and then glanced at the door. "Speaking of the devil, here he comes now."

Cherise's eyes swung over to the conference room door and her mouth went dry at the sight of Lee looking like his confident self. The dark blue suit molded every scrumptious inch of his tall, powerful body. His dark brown hair looked perfect and she knew how his eyes looked more blue than green until he was upset or turned on. *Shit!* This was going to be a long meeting.

She didn't miss how his gaze swung between her and David. She saw how Missy tried to step in front of him, but he went around her and headed straight for them. She willed herself to calm down and not embarrass herself.

"I better go. I don't feel like getting into an argument," David whispered the second before he left her and took a seat close to the head of the table.

Cherise opened her mouth and tried to yell for him to stay, but it was too late because she sensed Lee at her side. "You look very sexy this morning. I love how smooth and rich your skin looks in white. However, I think the skirt is a little short. I don't like other men staring at my woman's legs," Lee breathed in her ear making her nipples hardened underneath her shirt.

"I'm not your woman," she whispered under her breath as she crossed her arms over her breasts.

The sound of Justin Cane coming into the office stopped Lee from answering her. She started towards the last empty seat in the room, but Lee's hand snaked around her arm stopping her from moving. "I don't think so, sexy. You're staying here with me. I'm not going to let you sit next to your *friend*," Lee muttered, tugging her in front of his body.

The way Lee said the word friend it made her think he was jealous of David. Surely, he knew that she had no interest in him. "Let go of my arm."

"Not a chance," Lee said. "I want you to spend some time with me."

"I spend a lot of time with you. We're working on an assignment together, plus I see you at your house all the time."

"Cherise, for once can you just not argue and let me enjoy your company?" Lee asked as Justin Cane turned off the lights and started the DVD he wanted them to watch. She got a sneaky feeling that Lee was going to take advantage of this situation. They were the only ones in the back of the dark room and everyone else's attention was focused up front.

She sucked in a breath as she felt his fingers start to massage her stomach through her shirt. The heat from his touch sent a stream of moisture between her thighs. "Stop that," Cherise admonished, tugging at Lee's thick wrist. "We have to watch this."

"Babe, I own my marketing firm. I know how to do all of these things. I just took this job as something to keep me interested in my work. I'm sure I know more about this business than that video will tell me."

"Fine, then let me listen to it." She tried to move again, but Lee's grip only got tighter.

"You can hear fine from here."

Cherise stood in the crowded room and tried to play attention to the marketing plan DVD that her boss was playing, but she couldn't because all she could think about was how hot Lee's chest felt against her back.

She wondered what her co-workers would think if they knew Lee's cock was poking her in the lower part of her back. He was purposely trying to make her lose control since she brushed him off at breakfast a couple of days ago. She didn't have time to deal with his blatant come on because he wasn't serious about her. Lee only wanted her because she challenged him. Just the thought of making love to the hunk behind her made a low groan slip from between her lips.

"Sexy, are you okay?"

"Yes, I'm fine," she tossed back.

"I agree. You're fine as hell, but that's not what I was asking. You seem a little worked up. Is there something I can do to relieve your...stress?"

"Nope, I don't need your help at all."

"Oh, I don't believe you," Lee chuckled above her head the second before his hand raised up the back of her short skirt.

"What are you doing?" she hissed as the cool air hit her bare ass exposed by the g-string.

"Shit," he growled low enough for only her ears to hear. He rubbed his hand over her smooth bottom. "What brought on this change? Did you know how much I love touching a perfect ass in skimpy underwear?"

"It's none of your business," Cherise snapped, tugging at Lee's arm wrapped around her waist. "Get your hand off of me and pull my skirt back down before Mr. Cane turns the light back on and someone sees us."

"Cherise, every eye is glued to that damn video and if you stop moving around no one is going to look our way," Lee retorted as he eased two fingers inside of her body again for a second time in a two-week period.

"Isn't this where we left off in your office a few days ago? I think I was about to make you scream with pleasure before the level-headed side of you kicked in."

"Stop," she muttered, closing her eyes on the sweet pleasure Lee was causing in her body.

"Not this time, luscious," he answered, spreading her legs further apart with his knee. "While everyone else is learning how to run a perfect marketing campaign, I want you coming apart in my arms and all over my fingers."

Lord, she couldn't believe that the thought of having an orgasm with everyone around was turning her on her so much. What was it about Lee that brought out the *bad* side in her so much? This wasn't right. Someone was going to see them and then she would be out of a job.

"No."

"Yes," Lee countered, pushing his fingers in until he was knuckle deep. "Holy shit, you're so fucking hot," he murmured in her ear. "Now, I'm going to give you what you've been craving since the day I walked into your antique shop and you can't scream or you'll give us away."

"Lee, don't," she insisted, squirming around. "I won't be able to hold back."

"Yes, you will. Just think about how hot it will be every time we come back in this room knowing I gave you an orgasm right here in the back under the hanging plant. It will always be our little secret."

"I hate you," Cherise uttered.

"Not for long you won't," Lee promised, then took her ear between his teeth and nibbled as his fingers thrust in and out of her at a pace she didn't know was possible.

CLOSER TO YOU: LEE

# *Chapter Twelve*

Just as quickly as Lee started tormenting her, he stopped, shocking the hell out of her. One minute his thick fingers were inside of her, and in the next they were gone, and her skirt was pulled back down on her bare ass.

"What in the hell is going on?" she hissed, trying to calm down her heated body. Why would he stop and leave her like this?

"We're about to get some company," he hissed, stepping to the side. Shoving his hands into his pockets, Lee turned his attention away from her over to Missy, who was fast approaching them.

"Hey, Lee," Missy practically purred as she stepped next to them. "I saw you standing back here with Cherise and thought I would join you. You don't mind, do you?"

Cherise sneaked at peek at Lee from the corner of her eye and bit the inside of her mouth to keep from commenting. Missy wasn't talking to her so she left it alone.

"You're here now so there isn't much I can do about it," Lee commented.

The thought of standing there listening to Missy flirt with Lee turned her stomach. She didn't have the time or energy to deal with this. However, if Lee really wanted Missy's company over hers then she wasn't going to stand her and listen to them flirt back and forth.

"Why don't the two of you stay here and I'll go take Missy's seat next to David?" Cherise started past Lee and stopped when his hand wrapped around her arm. She glanced down at his touch and then looked back up into his eyes.

The jealousy she saw there surprised her. "Do you mind letting go of my arm?"

"There's no reason for you to leave," he stated.

"That's okay. I wanted to sit down and now I have the chance." She shook off Lee's touch and hurried over to the seat next to David. Cherise made sure that she didn't look back at Lee for the rest of the presentation.

God, why did she ever let the thought that Lee was truly interested in her enter her mind? Missy was the trophy arm piece men like her brother-in-law loved to show off to their friends. Well…that was the last time Lee would place his hands anywhere on her body. The next time he tried to touch her, he might just lose a finger.

\* \* \* \*

Lee watched as Cherise pretended he wasn't in the room. How could have things gone from being so good to so bad in a matter of seconds? She was responding to him like he always dreamt about and Missy had to come over and ruin it.

Did she really think that he wanted Missy? Cherise was the perfect woman in every sense of the word. All of her luscious curves were perfect for the loving he was dying to give her. He just had to find a way to seduce her into his bed. She was already living under the same roof as him. It was only a matter of time before he was between those sweet thighs of hers.

"Lee, are you listening to me?" Missy asked, running her nails down the middle of his chest. "I know you aren't interested in this video."

"Missy, I don't think we should talk through this. Mr. Cane is showing it for a reason." He had to find a way to get her off his back or Cherise wasn't going to give him the time of day. He wasn't dumb. He knew the history between the blonde and Cherise. They hated each other and he wasn't about to be pulled into the middle. He only had one interest, and that was getting his sexy-as-hell sister-in-law in his life.

"I'm sure he isn't paying any attention to us," she whispered as her hand slid down to his belt buckle. "I find you really hot and I would love to go out on a date with you."

Wrapping his fingers around Missy's bony wrist, Lee removed the unwanted hand from his body. "I think you should stop before I have a talk with Mr. Cane," he threatened. "I'm sure he doesn't want to lose me. My name alone is going to bring a lot of money to this firm."

He let go of Missy's hand as a look of utter disbelief crossed her face. Without looking in Cherise's direction, Lee made his way across the room and out the door. He needed some time to himself to think about a way to handle the conflicting situations with Missy and Cherise. One woman he was dying to get into his life and the other one he had no interest in whatsoever.

# Chapter Thirteen

"Alicia, I think you should give me a chance. You know that I've wanted to date you for months. Now that Max is out of the picture, I don't know why you won't give us a chance to get to know each other better," Brad said, staring at the woman next to him on the bench.

"Brad, you're a wonderful man. I like you a lot and I don't want to ruin our friendship by taking it to the next level. It's hard for me to have only guy friends and you're my best friend. Can't we just leave it at that?"

"No, I want more from you. I don't mind taking it slow, but I know you feel something for me more than friendship. I know you were jealous when you saw me dancing with Traci awhile ago." Caramel eyes glanced away from his and Alicia shrugged a slim shoulder. "I didn't think it was right the way you were dancing with her. She was your brother's girlfriend back then."

"Traci was and is my friend. Besides, I wasn't interested in my brother's woman. I only want you, but you aren't giving me an inch to work with. I'm sorry that Max turned out to be a jerk, but I'm a good guy and you know that."

"Brad, can we please drop this?" Alicia pleaded. "I can't let myself get involved with you. You're too good of a friend to lose and I won't do it." Twirling around, she snatched up her gym bag off the ground and raced out of the gate past Lee before he could stop her.

"Why is she always running away from you?" Lee asked, sitting down on the bench next to him.

"I honestly don't know," Brad mumbled. "I'm so in love with Alicia, but she doesn't want to mess up the friendship we have. I want so much more from her than that. Damn it, I'm not going to let her do this to us. I know she feels something for me. But she's scared to admit it."

"I thought she had feelings for that Max guy?"

"No, I'm beginning to think she was using him as a shield to hide from me. I know she wants me. After that one kiss we shared, I know the passion is there. All I have to do is bring it out."

"I wish you were this determined when it came to working at the office," Lee chuckled.

Brad looked at his brother and tried to keep his temper under control. "I don't want a lecture from you. Aren't you chasing after Cherise and she hates the sight of you? Why are you pushing yourself on a woman who doesn't want you?"

"Shut up, Brad!" Lee growled. "When it comes to my relationship with Cherise, it's my business and not yours."

A smirk tugged at the corners of Brad's mouth. "See...it doesn't feel good when the shoe is on the other foot, does it?" Squirming around on the bench, Lee glanced at him and then ran his fingers through his hair. "Sorry, I didn't mean to be such an asshole to you. I know how much you do care about Alicia."

"Thanks, but my feelings aren't returned. She constantly finds a way to run away from me or toss me into the friend category. I'm so fed up with that. If I wasn't so in love with her, I would have found someone else a long time ago," Brad sighed.

"Invite her over to the house for dinner."

"What?"

"Cherise is always making enough food for an army. She loves to think of new recipes and since we're having our weekly family dinner in a few days, bring Alicia along."

Brad let the idea roll over in his mind. "What good would it do? Alicia would only see it as a friend date and nothing more."

"I have a suggestion. How about we give Alicia a little test?" Lee suggested.

"What kind of test are you talking about? I don't want to scare her off."

"I think you should bring another one of your clients to dinner as your date and then ask Alicia what she thought of her."

"Okay. What if she doesn't care?" Brad asked.

"Brad, you're my brother and I love you, but you need to know where you stand with Alicia. You can't keep longing for her if she truly doesn't want you."

Brad hated to admit that Lee was right. He needed to figure out if Alicia would ever give the two of them a chance as a couple and if she didn't, then it was time to let her go.

"Okay, I'll do it."

"Alright, I'll let Cherise know when I get home tonight."

Brad had noticed how much Lee had changed since Cherise moved in with him. He was still surprised by the fact she had agreed to do it. They were like oil and water. Half the time the two of them didn't mixed too well together, but he got so much fun out of watching the two of them fight with each other.

"Are you sure that she won't mind cooking the meal?" He didn't want to force Cherise to do something that she didn't want to do.

"I know she'll love it," Lee replied.

"Great. I'll check and see if Alicia agrees and I'll let you know before Wednesday." Brad prayed that this would be the thing that finally got Alicia to open up her eyes and see that friends could make the best lovers and husbands. All he had to do was make her see it.

CLOSER TO YOU: LEE

# *Chapter Fourteen*

"Did I ever tell you how good you look in black?" A warm voice whispered by her ear before a kiss was placed beneath it. "Anytime you wear this color, I want to strip you naked and make love to you all night long."

Cherise shivered as Lee's words rolled over her body. Why did she always let him to this to her? What happened to the strong woman that pushed him away at every turn? He was making her into a puddle of emotions and that couldn't happen.

"Why don't you leave me alone?" she complained as she spun away from the sink and then gasped when a single rose was placed in front of her face.

"I'm sorry for what happened at work today. I shouldn't have even looked in Missy's direction."

"What makes you think I cared you paid attention to Missy?" she asked, taking the rose from Lee. He was too damn good looking for his own good.

Cupping her chin in his had, Lee tilted her head back under she could look into his eyes. "You cared and I'm sorry."

Licking her lips, she noticed how Lee's eyes got dark as they followed the movement of her tongue. "If you say so," she said and tried to remove her chin, but Lee tightened his grip.

"Tell me how I can make it up to you. I don't want you mad at me. I love coming home knowing that I haven't pissed you off."

"My feelings shouldn't matter. I'm only here until my pipes get fixed. Besides, we're family and family gets on each others nerves from time to time."

Letting go of her face, Lee placed his hands on the sink behind them blocking her in with his massive body. He was making her want him and she wanted to hate it but she didn't.

"When are you going to stop pretending that there isn't more between us?" Lee asked as he ran his tongue along side of her earlobe. "My cock gets so hard when I get around you. All I can think about is making you scream as I come inside of you. I want you so bad that I wake up during the middle of the night drenched in sweat."

"You're lying," she whispered.

"Do you want proof?" Taking her hand, Lee laid it against the front of his slacks, wrapping her fingers around his erection.

It felt wonderfully hot and thick to her hand. She couldn't resist the urge to give it a nice squeeze. "You're so...." She was at a loss for words.

"Baby, your touch feels so damn good. I bet it would even feel better without any clothes between us."

Leaning closer, Cherise got lost in the moment as the rose slipped from her fingers and landed on the floor. "Do you really think so?"

Lee's bluish-green eyes clashed with hers as he stared at her. "Sunshine, I know that it would. Do you want to test it out?"

The word yes was on the tip of her tongue as the sound of the front door slamming shut echoed through the house followed by the sound of Richard's voice. "Lee, are you home? I need to talk to you."

Cherise froze as the reality of the situation set in. She was in the kitchen with her hand wrapped around Lee's cock. What would be going on if Richard had walked in five minutes later? Embarrassment burned her cheeks as she snatched back her hand, shoved Lee away from her and picked up the rose off the floor.

"This can't happen again," she whispered, stepping around Lee's body a second before Richard strolled into the room. He paused and looked at her then at Lee standing behind her.

"Hey guys! What's going on?"

"Nothing," she muttered as she made her way around Richard and out of the room. Cherise felt Richard and Lee staring at her, but she didn't look back. She couldn't let Lee see how bad their little rendezvous bothered her.

\* \* \* \*

"Okay…spill it. What did I miss? Where you about to have your way with her on the table? From the look on her face, I'm guessing that I got pretty close," Richard said.

Lee wanted to shove his brother back out the door and follow Cherise upstairs. She was so close to giving in to him and Richard had to show up and ruin it. Shit, he was never going to get Cherise in his life and bed if people kept popping up uninvited all the time.

"You didn't miss a damn thing," he sighed, trying to block out the throbbing erection in his pants.

"Yeah right," Richard laughed. "We all know that you have wanted the lovely Cherise ever since you laid eyes on her. It's almost funny that she doesn't know how much you already care about her."

Lee knew that he wasn't good at keeping his feelings hid for Cherise, but it couldn't be that bad. Was it and he didn't know it? "Cherise is just acting like she always does."

"Why are you lying?" Richard asked, pulling out a chair at the table, he took a seat.

"I'm not lying," Lee denied, joining his brother at the table. "Anyways, I'm tired of talking about myself. What's going on with you? Have you finally gotten Dawn to agree to a wedding date?"

"No, she's still fighting me on that. I can't get her to believe that I've gotten over that damn tape. She's with me and I know she loves me, but the marriage thing is scaring her off."

"Why?" Lee asked concerned. "Did she lie to you? Was she really upset that you showed us that dumb ass tape? Doesn't she understand that we don't hold it against her? Everyone makes mistakes and I have seen worse things than that tape? Her ex-boyfriend was an asshole for even trying to blackmail her with it anyway."

"No. She's scared since *D4* is such a success now that if she marries me and her past comes out, it will hurt the restaurant," Richard replied.

"Are you worried? Are you willing for all of that to come out?"

"I love having *D4*, but Dawn is my world. I'll sell it to Hamilton if that means Dawn will walk down the aisle to me."

Lee practically fell out of his seat. Richard hated Hamilton and tried to get Dawn away from him at every turn. "You really wouldn't do that, would you?"

"Yes, if it meant that Dawn believed that *D4* doesn't mean more than her," Richard sighed. "I watch her sleep at night and I know I can't make it without her being my wife. She's *everything* to me."

He heard the passion in Richard's voice about Dawn and knew his brother was serious. "Richard, Dawn wouldn't want you to give up *D4* for her. Why don't you just talk her through her fears and I'm sure that everything will be okay. She's a wonderful woman."

"I know she is," Richard whispered lovingly. "I love her so much. I almost lost her and I was lucky enough to get her back. Now, I can't get her to take that final step with me. Do you think it's me?"

Lee frowned at his brother's comment. "I can't believe you asked me that. Dawn loves you and there's nothing wrong with you except your jealousy issues. Tell her how you're truly feeling."

"It has been a while since we had a romantic dinner and talked to each other. She's always so busy helping Hamilton and I'm at *D4* until after midnight. I think I need to change that."

"Sounds like you do. You don't want to lose Dawn again because of work coming between the two of you." He wished his problems with Cherise was that easy to fix.

"I think I'm going to surprise her at work and take her out to eat and maybe dancing. I heard her talking about this new band she wants to hear," Richard said, standing up. "I'm leaving. I want to catch Dawn before she gets involved in something." Richard paused at the table and looked at him. "Don't give up on Cherise. The two of you are meant to be together. Just find a way to make her see it. I can tell you're getting to her."

"How do you know that?" he sighed.

"There's no way the old Cherise would have stayed here with you. She would have stayed at her house and found a way to deal with her water problem. All you have to do is stop coming on so strong and things should fall into place."

"I'll think about it," Lee replied.

"That's all I ask." Richard waved at him and then spun on his heel and left him alone with his thoughts.

"Take it slow? Can I really do that when it comes to Cherise?" he asked aloud as he heard the love of his life moving around upstairs in her bedroom. "I guess I can try, but if it doesn't work, I'm going back to my old ways. Cherise isn't going to be moving back to her house when those pipes are fixed. She's already home, even if she doesn't realize it yet."

# Chapter Fifteen

The smell of food cooking woke Cherise up early the next morning. She lay in bed and wondered who was cooking breakfast on a Saturday, because Lee let his staff have the weekends off. Stretching, she debated on whether or not she wanted to stay in bed or get out. However, the growling in her stomach made the decision for her.

Tossing the covers off her body, she grabbed her robe from the foot of the bed, put it on and tied it around her waist. Cherise made her way out of her bedroom and down the stairs to the kitchen. She was falling in love with Lee's house. It was like a mansion, but it had all the touches of home. She saw all of his childhood memories throughout the house and it brought a smile to her face.

Lee wasn't as tough as he came off and that's why it was getting harder for her to fight her growing attraction to him. He was always catching her off guard with a kiss here and there. He was starting to make her believe that he honestly didn't care about her weight, but she was still trying to lose some pounds. Traci didn't know about it and she wasn't about to tell her sister. She knew without a doubt that she would be a knockout if she were a little thinner.

She stopped in her tracks in the kitchen doorway at the sight of Lee in a pair of black boxers and nothing else. Shit, the fabric hugged his tight ass like nobody's business. Licking her lips, she placed her hand over her heart and tried to calm down her racing hormones. She wasn't some love struck teenager anymore. Those days were long gone and she was happy about it too.

"Do you need any help?" Was that her voice that sounded that breathless?

Lee added several strips of bacon to the skillet before he looked over his shoulder at her. "Good morning, Cherise. No, I don't need any help, but thanks for the offer." Spinning back around, he broke open a couple of eggs and dropped them into a silver mixing bowl at his elbow.

Cherise frowned as she came further into the room? Where was the real Lee and who in the hell was this imposter? There was no way Lee wouldn't have a sexually filled comeback to her question. It just wasn't like him and she hated to admit she was a little disappointed.

"Are you sure?" she asked, standing at his side.

"Yeah, I'm sure. How about you take a shower and get dressed. I should have the food done by then," he answered without looking at her.

Grabbing Lee by the arm, she spun him around to face her. She swallowed down a moan as her eyes landed on his bare chest and amazing abs. "What's wrong with you? Last night you were trying to seduce me into your bed and now you're acting like nothing happened?"

"Nothing is wrong," Lee replied, looking at her. "I've just decided to take your advice. Maybe we should just be in-laws and nothing more."

Cherise swallowed down her hurt and took a step back from Lee. "I was right about you. You weren't really interested in dating the fat chick. What was it? Were you just trying to see how far you could get with me? Would the fat, lonely me lose her mind because the handsome Lee Drace showed her some attention?" She practically spat the words at him.

Lee turned off the burner and narrowed his eyes at her. "How many times do I have to tell you how perfect your body is?"

"Save it, Lee. I can't take anymore of your lies." Cherise gave Lee a hard look before turning away from him. She had only made it halfway across the room before she had him mumble behind her.

"Damn it! I'm so tired of this." A strong hand wrapped around her arm and twirled her back around. She didn't have a chance to say a word before Lee's mouth slammed down on hers.

Everything around her seemed to stop as Lee moved her body backwards and her back hit the wall. His tongue was inside of her mouth, dominating her, and the wanton side of her loved every minute. She didn't have any time to think as Lee moved her away from the wall and stripped the robe from her body.

"You're so damn beautiful," he growled as his eyes raked over her chest in the sheer bra that stopped a little below her breasts. It wasn't much support for her double D's, but she loved how sexy it made her feel.

"You're lying," she moaned as Lee pressed his thick cock between her legs. If the wall hadn't been supporting her, she would have fallen to the floor.

"Babe, I'm not lying to you," he growled as his lips wrapped around a hard nipple and sucked it into his moist mouth.

Moisture pooled between her legs, soaking her underwear, she slid her fingers through Lee's hair and held him against her aching breast. "Oh, that feels so good," she moaned.

Lee let go of her nipple with a pop. "It will only get better," he promised as he tore her underwear from her body and inserted two fingers.

Her orgasm hit her so fast that all Cherise could do was ride it out. Lee muttered encouraging words against her neck as she came all over his fingers and hand. "Tell me to stop and I will, but if you don't, I'm going to make love to you. I can't wait any longer. I need to be inside of you. I want to feel your tightness wrapped around my cock as I come inside of you."

She didn't even think about it a second before she muttered. "I want you, too." For once in her life, she was going to do something without overanalyzing it first.

Cherise didn't have time to regain her breath before Lee had them both stripped naked and he was sitting in a kitchen chair, easing her down on his impressive cock. She shivered at the feel of him inside of her. "Oh, you're so thick," she moaned as Lee picked up the pace of his thrusts.

"Only for you, Sunshine," he growled as his body started to get slick with sweat and his mouth latched onto her nipple.

Screaming, she wrapped her hands around his biceps as Lee slid her up and down on his erection with slow determined thrusts. The only sounds in the room were the clock ticking behind them on the wall and the purrs mingled with groans as Lee worked on giving her another release that her body needed.

Letting go of her breast, he blew at her nipple causing it to get even harder. Cherise bit her lip to keep from screaming out. Being like this with Lee was so much better than she ever imagined and he wasn't acting like her extra pounds bothered him at all. In fact, his gripped tightened on her hips like he was never going to let her go.

"Confess," he breathed by her ear and then ran his tongue down the side of her neck.

"Confess to what?" she panted as Lee's erection throbbed inside of her weakening body. Her orgasm was so close she could fell it.

"That you were attracted to me…"

"Yeah…sure," she panted.

Lee voice rumbled deep in his throat as he held her hips and stopped their movement. "That's not what I want."

She squirmed around trying to get Lee to finish what he had started. Her body was burning with the need to explode. "Please," Cherise begged. It had been so long and she needed this.

"Is this what you want?" Lee asked, sliding her half way up his penis and then back down.

"Yes," she panted as sweat poured down her back and the ends of her hair brushed the top of her shoulders.

"Well…that is all you're going to get unless you answer my question."

Cherise's tawny eyes clashed with Lee's every changing blue ones. She saw that he was fighting for control the way the muscle twitched in his jaw. He wanted this as much or more than she did. Could she admit to that tiny piece of information to get what she wanted? *Hell yeah!*

"Yes, I was attracted to you the first day I meet you in my antique shop," she confessed licking her bottom lip. "You were all I thought about for the rest of the day."

Triumph flashed in Lee's eyes as a cocky smile pulled at the corners of his mouth. "Good girl," he growled before he gave one final thrust sending them both over the edge.

Gasping, Cherise let her head drop against Lee's shoulder as her body slowly came back down from the high that it was on. She felt good as Lee stood up and carried her from the room, but she was too exhausted to say a word.

A few minutes later, her back touched the softness of a mattress and Lee climbed in the bed next to her, placing her head on his chest. His heart thundered loudly under her ear and she wondered what was going to happen between the two of them now. Did he think that this changed their relationship? Was he looking for a commitment or just another body to keep his bed warm? How in the hell could she let this happen?

Cherise tried to rise, but Lee pushed her back down on his chest. "You know this doesn't change a thing between us," she whispered, placing her hand over his heart.

"It was just a dream," Lee mumbled above her as his fingers slid through her hair and his breathing slowed down as sleep started to take over. "Now, go to sleep."

# *Chapter Sixteen*

"What's wrong with you?"

Cherise shoved her barely touched plate of lasagna away from her and stared at her sister who was sitting across from her at *D4*. Traci had wanted to have lunch with her since they both hadn't seen each other in about two weeks. She was happy to see her baby sister and nephew, but she couldn't get her mind off what happened between her and Lee.

"Nothing is wrong. I just have been busy working with Lee on the marketing thing and that's about it," she lied, hoping Traci would drop it.

"I know you too well. You're hiding something from me and I want to know what it is."

"Why would you say that?"

"Your whole body is acting like you have a secret, but you can't tell me," Traci replied, drumming her fingers on the restaurant table. "Come clean. You know that I'll find out sooner or later."

"It's nothing."

An eyebrow arched over her sister's eyes and Traci studied her like she was on trial. "Does it have anything to do with Lee?"

"No," Cherise snapped a little too loudly and then cursed under her breath when a smile spread across her sister's face.

"I knew it. Zack mentioned something about how Lee seemed more relaxed now and not as uptight. What happened between the two of you in that huge house of his?"

"Nothing," Cherise mumbled, looking away. She felt her face getting hotter by the minute.

"Oh my God, you slept with him, didn't you?" Traci whispered. "Was it good? Are you sharing his bed now? Are the two of you a couple? Should I start planning a wedding?"

She thought about lying as she looked at her sister, but knew it wouldn't do any good. Traci already knew her secret and wouldn't stop bugging her until she admitted the truth. "Yes, I slept with Lee."

"Was it good?" Traci grinned.

"It was unbelievable," Cherise said softly and hated that she wished it would happen again.

"I knew it. You're in love with him. Cherise, why don't you tell him? I know that Zack said Lee had some pretty strong feelings towards you."

*I'm not in love with Lee*, she thought.

"You're wrong. It was just sex and nothing more," Cherise sighed with a shake of her head. "A lapse in judgment or something like that. You know that can happen sometimes."

"You keep telling yourself that, but I'm not going to believe it. Lee has been sniffing around you for a while. I think if you had started dating him back then, you would be married to him by now. He wants you, big sister."

"He had me and now it's over. I don't want to discuss it anymore. Besides, don't you have to go in the back and steal Carter back from Richard? I didn't get to spend anytime with my nephew before he took him away."

Traci laughed causing her spiral curls to bounce up and down on her shoulders. "You're just too much. When I was dating Zack, you had all kinds of advice about him. Now that you're with Lee, I can't tell you a thing."

"I'm not with Lee," Cherise hissed and then calmed down. "It was just a moment of passion and it isn't going to happen again."

Standing up, Traci gave her one long look. "You better not make him wait too long or someone else is going to take him away from you. Lee may come across as strong, but he isn't. He wants love and he thinks he can get it from you. If you honestly don't want anything to do with him, then you need to tell him."

Cherise sat in her seat and thought about what Traci said as her sister walked towards Richard's office. She loved her sister, but Traci didn't understand that she could never be the trophy piece that Lee needed in his life.

Now, she thought she was an attractive looking woman and men did look at her. However, men who looked like Lee Drace never gave her a passing glance, so she wasn't going to let a hot moment of sex cloud her mind. Lee wanted her and now that he had her, things were over between them. He would go and find someone like Amanda or Missy to warm his bed.

"I was weak once, but I won't be weak again," Cherise promised herself as she got up and left the restaurant without saying goodbye, or seeing the baby.

# Chapter Seventeen

Lee wondered how long Cherise thought he was going to sit there and listen to her tell him why they shouldn't make love again. She was in his blood now and he wasn't about to let her go. The reason she hadn't been in his bed again was out of respect. He didn't want her to think she was only a warm body for him. She was so much more and he was going to prove it to her.

"I just wanted to let you know where I stand with this. As soon as I find another place to live, I'm going to move out. I don't think it would be right if we stayed under the same roof."

"Is that so?" he asked, leaning back in his chair. He was supposed to meet Cherise at her job in an hour, but she came here to see him first. Most of his staff had gone out to lunch and he was dying to be with Cherise again. The door was closed and no one came into his office without his knowing. He wondered how quickly he could have Cherise stripped out of that red dress and be buried deep inside of her.

He ran his hand over his cock and tried to get some relief, but it wasn't working. Ever since Cherise came into his office, he had been hard and ready to go. "I don't think I agree with you."

Cherise blinked at him and then stood up. "I didn't ask you to agree with me. I was just telling you how it is." She turned away from him and made her way for the door.

Jumping up from his seat, he raced after her stopping her before her hand touched the doorknob. "Do you know what I want to agree to?" he whispered by her ear as he reached out and locked the door.

"I don't care what you want," she snapped, but ruined it by shivering when he brushed his erection against her ass.

"I bet you do care, Sunshine."

"That's what you think."

Spinning her around, Lee pressed Cherise's warm body against the door with his. He loved how her curves fit to him perfectly. If there had been a woman made especially for him, it was Cherise Roberts.

He dropped his head and slowly ran the tip of his tongue along side the edge of her mouth. "Open for me. I want to taste you."

Cherise shook her head and tried to shove him away, but he wasn't having any of that. He couldn't go back to the way things used to be between them. After knowing how her body fit his like a glove, he was going to be spending a lot of time in it.

"Fine, I can find a better place to use my tongue then." Lee quickly undid the belt that was keeping Cherise's dress together and dropped it to the floor. He smiled at the sight her of lacey black bra and matching underwear. Without giving her a chance to think, he quickly tore at the barely-there material covering her wetness from him.

Dropping down to his knees, he spread her legs apart and ran his tongue across her drenched entrance. "Tasty, I think I want another sample." Lee picked Cherise up and carried her over to the couch and got back between her spread thighs. The scent of her arousal was driving him crazy.

"Lee…we can't."

"I can do any damn thing I want and I want this," he growled before he got back down to business.

The sound of Cherise moaning his name filled his ears, pushing him on as he felt her body tense up, he quickly got up and tore off his clothes. He couldn't let Cherise come without him. Picking her up, he lay down on the couch at the same time be brought her down on his throbbing cock. The motion shattered the both of them over the edge. Lee caught Cherise's mouth with his and swallowed down her scream as he emptied his seed into her waiting body.

His heart swelled even more with love for the woman above him when she rested her head on his chest and snuggled closer. Cherise might not be in love with him, but he knew with a little more of this that she might start seeing things his way.

"This is so wrong. We are so wrong for each other," her soft voice whispered against his chest.

Lee couldn't stop his hands from running down her back and cupping her plump ass in his hands. He could make love to Cherise any way he wanted without the fear he would hurt her. He wasn't about to let her talk herself out of being with him. He had been waiting too fucking long for this.

"Let's not go there. How about we just take things slowly and see where we end up. Who knows we might end up having something like my brother and Traci have."

Cherise pushed herself up and looked at him. "You think that we can get married to each other? Half the time we're at each other throats and when we aren't….."

"I'm making you come apart in my arms," he grinned, then winked. "Sunshine, you're going to be mine and I'm not going to stop until it happens."

"Okay," came the soft reply as Cherise pushed herself off his chest and then got up.

He laid there and watched Cherise while she got dressed. He wished that she would open up to him more. She was such a strong and opinionated woman, but he could see the sadness in her gorgeous eyes. He had to find a way to make that go away. Lee was certain a man had hurt her in the past. Now he just had to find out how to undo the damage that person had done or he'll never truly have a chance with her.

"Have dinner with me," he blurted out.

Tying the belt around her waist, Cherise shook her head. "I can't do that. I already have plans."

"With whom?" he growled, jumping up from the couch. He was tired of Cherise finding ways to avoid him after they made love. He wasn't her sexual play toy.

"I'm meeting with a new client tonight and I can't be late. He's going out of town for a week and I need to get with him."

"No."

The fire he loved seeing flashed in Cherise's eyes as she crossed her arms under her breasts. "Did you tell me no?"

"Damn right. You aren't having dinner with some man. I barely tolerate your relationship with David."

"Lee, you have no say in what I do," she snapped, trying not to look at his naked body.

"Honey, please stop shoving people between us," he whispered as he slid his hand through her hair and kissed her lightly on the mouth. "I'm interested in you and I don't want to share you with other men."

"I'm not shoving anyone between us, Lee. I had this dinner planned weeks ago. This could be the biggest client I ever had. It could be the job I need to help me open my own catering business. You already took my antique shop away from me. Don't take this, too."

Pain pierced Lee's heart as he stepped back from Cherise. He *knew* it. She still hated him for making her sign over that property to Zack. Running his hand down his face, he shook off his sadness and started picking up his clothes off the floor. He felt Cherise watching him, but he didn't say a word until he was completely dressed.

"I'm sorry that you haven't gotten over that Ms. Roberts, but I can promise I won't stand in the way of anymore of your dreams. I'll see you later." Lee walked over to the door and unlocked it. He went out without looking back at Cherise, who was standing in the middle of the room.

# *Chapter Eighteen*

"I need to speak with you for a moment," Traci said behind him, but it came out as more of a demand than a request.

Placing his drink back down on the table, Lee turned around in his chair and looked at his spunky sister-in-law with his adorable nephew on her hip. He reached for the baby and took him from Traci. Carter grinned at him and then stuck his fat little fist inside of his mouth. It pained him that he would never have a family with Cherise.

"What can I do for you?"

"I want to know why you're messing with my sister. Cherise isn't here for you to use and toss away. She has feelings despite the fact she doesn't show them all of the time."

"I haven't done anything to her," he denied. "She's the one that doesn't want a relationship with me. I ask her out to dinner and she turns me down. I thought once we were under the same roof that things would change, but I was wrong."

"Things have changed because you've slept with her. As far as I know of, my sister hasn't been interested in anyone since Chad."

Lee didn't ask how Traci knew he was having sex with Cherise because something else more important caught his attention. "Who in the hell is Chad?"

Rolling her eyes, Traci fell down into the seat next to him and brushed a lock of Carter's dark hair off his forehead. The baby grinned at her and then went back to sucking his fist.

"Chad is Cherise's ex-boyfriend, and he did a real number on her. I never thought she would be interested in a man again until you came along. I knew the minute she mentioned your name that she liked you. She got this look in her eyes that I had never seen before."

"What did this bastard do to her?"

"Lee, watch your language when you're holding my son," Traci scolded.

"Sorry," he apologized and then kissed Carter on the cheek. His nephew removed his wet hand from his mouth and touched him on the side of the face. He couldn't hold back the love for the sweet baby he held in his arms. "He's just so cute. I was hoping..."

"You were hoping what?" Traci asked, taking Carter away from him.

He wiped off his face with the back of his hand and then shook his head. "It doesn't matter now. Tell me more about Chad. What did he do to Cherise?"

"He was a real jerk. Chad constantly picked on Cherise about her weight. He told her a real man wouldn't want a woman who was fat and worked long days. He tried several times to get her to sell the shop and stay at home."

"That's what she meant," Lee mumbled under his breath as the pieces started coming together. Cherise didn't believe he wanted her to have a career. God, he had to shake some sense into that gorgeous head of hers.

"Who is *she* and what did *she* mean?" Traci asked.

"Nothing, I just found out something that might help me get what I want after all. I need to talk to Cherise."

"You can't."

Lines popped out in the middle of Lee's forehead as he glanced at Traci. "What do you mean I can't? Cherise should be at home by now. I'm headed there so I can talk to her. We need to get a few things out in the open."

"You can go back to your house, but you won't find Cherise there. She called me from the airport." "Why is she at the airport? Is she leaving me?" Lee hoped that Traci didn't notice his slip, but the huge grin on her face told him that she had.

"No, the guy she is catering the party for wanted her to meet him there. He was running late and he suggested she talk with him in his limo on the way to his hotel."

"Cherise is going to a hotel with some guy she doesn't know?" Lee sputtered, getting up from his seat. "Has she lost her mind? Wait until I get my hands on her."

"You aren't going to do a thing," Traci exclaimed, standing up. "Cherise is a grown woman and she knows what she's doing. She isn't going to put herself in any kind of danger. So, why don't you think of a different approach to win my sister over?"

Lee wanted to be mad, but he couldn't. Traci was right. Cherise was an intelligent woman and she wouldn't put herself in harm's way. "You're right. I over reacted."

"I'm glad that you agree," Traci smiled. "Now tell your nephew goodbye. I have to get home and fix your brother something to eat."

Lee ran his hand over the baby's soft hair and kissed him on the cheek. "Bye, Carter. You be good for your mother."

"Oh, he's the sweetest baby. I never have a problem out of him." Kissing him on the cheek, Traci gave him a quick hug. "Don't worry, my sister will come around. Just be a little more patient with her," she whispered in his ear before she stepped back, turned and went out the door.

* * * *

Cherise unlocked the front door and eased inside the house, closing the door softly behind her. Her meeting with the new client went a lot longer than she thought, but

114

the advance he just paid her was well worth it. Placing her keys in the dish by the door, she made her way towards the stairs when a light coming of Lee's study drew her attention. She headed over to the door and took a deep breath. He was probably waiting up for her to give her the third degree. He had been in a foul mood since the last time they made love.

She couldn't believe that she let that happen again. When it came to Lee Drace and that deep coaxing voice of his, she found it so hard to tell him no. He was sneaking his way into her heart just like she knew he would and it wasn't fair. It wasn't like he could disappear from her life if things didn't work out between the two of them.

Her sister was married to his brother, which meant they were stuck with each for the rest of their lives, because she didn't think Traci was about to leave the love of her life.

Sending up a silent prayer, she pushed open the door and went inside shutting the door behind her. The sight she found surprised the hell out of her. Lee was stretched out on the big black leather couch sound asleep with an open book on the floor. He must have fallen asleep waiting for her.

Coming over to the table, she sat down and brushed a lock of hair off his forehead. Lee was hands down one of the best-looking men she had ever laid eyes on. His blue-green eyes seemed to follow her every move and the thick dark brown hair made her fingers itch to touch it. Plus, the dimple in his chin only added to his sex appeal. Why did a man she wanted more than anything in the world have to be her worst enemy?

"I can't fall in love with you. You'll just break my heart and I won't let that happen. Right now, I'm happy with what I have in my life. I can't ever let you know how I feel. Because you would just smile and blow it off with a cute comment. It's better that I let you go on thinking that I hate you."

Cherise grabbed the blanket off the back of the couch and covered Lee with it. She looked at him a few more minutes before she went out the door, but if she had looked back, she would have seen a pair of eyes following her.

# *Chapter Nineteen*

"I don't want to be just friends with you. You know how I feel and I'm not going to stop until you give me a chance. Will you at least have dinner at my brother Lee's house? He wants to get to know you better. All of my family will be there."

"I can't do it Brad," Alicia answered. "I'm not ready to jump into another relationship with anyone. I poured so much of myself into my relationship with Max and he just used me. I need time to heal from that." Brad wanted to be patient and give Alicia the time she needed, but he knew a lot of that was just a shield she was putting between then. She hadn't been in love with Max like she thought she had. Max was a user and now he was gone out of her life. He couldn't have asked for anything better. Now, he had to get her to see him for the man he was and not the tennis instructor who became her friend.

"You've been there before and not had a problem. Why can't you do it again? You'll have a lot of fun watching Lee drool over Cherise. Anyway, he invited you and he'll be very insulted if you didn't show up."

"I'm not sure," Alicia hedged. "Are you going to tell him that we're more than just friends?"

He wanted to jerk Alicia to him and kiss him until she realized that they were more than good buddies, but he could be patient. It took Zack a while win over Traci and the same thing with Richard and Dawn. Lee was in a constant battle with Cherise, so he didn't mind waiting his turn because Alicia was worth it.

If he had to go the friend's route and then sneak up on her, he'll do that. Because in the end, he knew that Alicia would be his wife. All he had to do was show her that she was worth everything that he wanted to give her. Ms. Alicia Hart didn't know what he had in store for her, so she better watch out. Once he set his sights on something, he was like his older brothers. He didn't give up until he got it.

"Sure, I'll tell my family we're just friends and I'm helping you through a difficult time. I'd rather be in your life as a friend than not at all," he lied.

An indescribable looked passed over Alicia's face as she looked back at him; it was almost like she was a little upset he wasn't fighting her over the friends thing. Well, she didn't have to worry. He wasn't going to keep living this lie for long.

"Do you think you can be at Lee's house around six o'clock tomorrow?"

"I'm pretty sure. I don't have to work, so I'll be there," Alicia answered.

"Would you rather me pick you up instead?" Brad inquired.

Alicia shook her head. "No, because I might have to leave early and I'd rather have my own car."

"Has anyone told you that you work too many hours? You're already a famous news reporter. You don't have to work yourself into the ground. You should be out having fun."

"You sound like my mother," she smiled. "I don't have much of a social life anymore, so my work is all that I have. I love the long hours." Brad kept his mouth closed. He wasn't about to let his secret out. After a few more dates with him, thinking about work would be the last thing on Alicia's mind. All her thoughts were going to be filled with him and how much they make each other happy.

"Okay, I'll see you at my brother's and just wear something causal," Brad said. He was debating on how he was going to keep his hands off Alicia until she got over of the idea of them being just friends.

# Chapter Twenty

"Do you really think that we can make money with an online catalog? I know it was my marketing plan, but I'm getting a little nervous about it now."

"Sunshine, it was a brilliant idea. Most people are computer literate now and an online shopping catalog is perfect, especially if we give it a fresh new look with lower shipping and handling. I know most customers want to purchase items from magazines, but the shipping and handling is what stops them," Lee said, pointing to the notes he took last night.

Cherise scooted closer to Lee and looked at the legal pad. They had decided to eat lunch in the conference room and work on her marketing plan some more today. Between her working on her other projects, worrying about the repairs at her house and getting ready for this huge catering job, they hadn't much time to sit down and talk things out.

"This is all that I found on the internet a couple of days ago, but I'm going to look some more. I have a couple of other places that I want to search first."

Cherise could barely keep her eyes open. She was so tired. All of this extra work was getting to her. It was even taking away some of her appetite, which in her opinion wasn't a bad thing. In the last month, she had lost about fifteen pounds and she thought that she was looked pretty good.

"Are you getting enough to eat?" Lee blurted out of the blue, shocking her.

"Why are you asking me that?"

"I just noticed you only took a couple bites of your sandwich and you didn't even touch your fries. Are you trying to lose weight or something?"

"No, I just wasn't as hungry as I thought I was, plus I have a lot going on right now. I'm fine, really. We're living under the same roof. Don't you see me eating the same meals as you?"

Lee eyed her for a couple of minutes. "Cherise, you know that you're perfect just the way you are. I wouldn't want you to change one thing about your gorgeous body. In fact, I was wondering when I might get another sample of it. I miss having you in my arms."

Her body burned at Lee's words, but they couldn't sleep together again. It would only make it harder for them in the end.

"I've already discussed this with you. We can't sleep together again. It wouldn't turn out good in the end."

"That's what you say, but what about what I want and need. You're the woman for me. I know this just like Zack and Richard knew. You can keep running from me all you want, but in the end you will have my ring on your finger."

Cherise couldn't take anymore of this. Lee was pressuring her with all of his talk about forever. Why couldn't he just leave well enough alone? Getting up, she tossed her pen down on the table. "I need to leave and get some fresh air. I'll meet you back at my office in about thirty minutes." She hurried out of the room before she changed her mind.

\* \* \* \*

"How are things going with you? You don't seem like yourself. Is there something going on between you and Cherise?" Zack turned over the steaks while he watched his brother from the corner of his eye.

"Cherise is the same as always. She's fighting me at every corner about her feelings for me. I thought once she got under the same roof as me, I could make her see we belonged together."

"I think Cherise has changed a lot towards you. Traci told me about what happened between the two of you."

"I don't what you're talking about," Lee hedged.

"Do you really want me to spell it out for you?"

"You might have to." Lee wasn't about to offer up any information that he wasn't sure that Zack already might know about. His brother was very good at getting stuff out of people without them knowing it.

"Traci told me that you slept with Cherise. Is that true? I'm surprise that it hadn't happen before now. The two of you always find a way to heat up a room."

"Yeah, it's true," Lee answered as he ran his hand across his hair. "It was damn good and now Cherise is trying to act like it never happened. I can't let her do that."

"Cherise is so stubborn and willful. She's totally the type of woman you need to calm you down, but are you willingly to fight for her? The two of you look so good together."

"I'm more than willingly to fight for her, but she has to stop shoving up these road blocks all the time. At work, she's all business and keeps a respectful distance away from me. At home, she finds ways not to interact with me unless it's necessary. God, I want to shake some sense into her." "I know that the last guy she dated turned out to be a real asshole, but I'm not going to hurt her like he did. I love her so much. I just want her to open up her heart to me and let me in."

"I can't believe it," Zack chuckled beside him.

"What's so damn funny?"

"My big brother is in love. I remember a time when you told me there wasn't a woman in the world who would get a ring from you. Now you want to give the woman a ring and she's running the other way."

"Zack, it isn't funny. I love Cherise and I have to find a way to get her to trust me enough to tell me her feelings."

Lee didn't know how he was going to do it, but before his time was up at Crane's, Cherise was going to be wearing his ring. He couldn't think about her moving out of his house. He liked walking into a room and smelling the scent of her perfume there. The little feminine touches in his home now warmed his heart.

Zack was right. Years ago, he would have laughed at the man he was today, but now he was torn up that he wasn't already married to the gorgeous woman not twenty feet away from him.

"Don't worry about it. You're going to get Cherise. I can see the change in her since she started living with you," Zack said next to him. "She doesn't have that hardness about her that she used to. She smiles a lot more now, too."

"Do you really think that has to do with me?"

"Sure do. How can she not laugh more when see has to see your ugly face every morning?" His brother joked, placing the steaks from the grill onto the plate next to him.

"You may think that, but Traci doesn't. She told me I really looked handsome tonight," Lee tossed back just to pick at Zack.

"You better be glad Traci is my wife or I might get upset by that comment. Besides, I know Cherise is the one who you want to give you a compliment."

"You're right about that. Why doesn't she laugh with me like that?" he asked, watching how Brad had Cherise and Traci laughing at something while he held Carter.

"Man, come on. You know Brad is trying to ease the hurt of Alicia not showing up at the last minute," Zack said.

"Did she stand him up on purpose?"

"No, her boss called her about a new breaking story he wanted her to cover. She called Brad from her car on the way to the news station."

"Brad hasn't looked at another woman since Alicia came into his life. I'm not sure if she's the woman for him. She keeps playing with his emotions all the time. I was thinking about having a talk with him," Lee confessed.

"I wouldn't do that if I was you. Remember how bad it turned out when you tried to have your talk with me about Traci?"

"Hey, I'm the oldest and I was only looking out for you."

"Let Brad figure out things for himself. I like Alicia and I think she'll be good for Brad, but our baby brother needs to figure out how to go after what he wants."

Lee got the hint that Zack was tossing his way. He wasn't ever going to get Cherise unless he started showing her more how much he wanted her. "I get your point," he said. "I'll go and see if I can get my tempting sister-in-law to spend some time with me."

"Good. I thought I might have to shove you in her direction. While you're over there, tell my wife to come and keep me company."

"Will do," Lee said. He left Zack and made his way over to Cherise. Her back was to him so she couldn't see him coming, because if she did, she would make a break for it.

Wrapping his arms around Cherise's waist, he planted a kiss on the back of her neck. She tried to squirm out of his grip, but he wasn't letting her go. "Go walking on the trail with me. I want to talk to you."

"I can't. I'm talking to Brad and Traci."

"Hey, I need to go and call Alicia. I want to see if she will go out for drinks with me after work," Brad said, handling Carter back to Traci. He grinned at them and then left.

124

"Traci, Zack wants you to come over to the grill and keep him company," Lee said relaying his brother's message and getting rid of Cherie's other excuse not to be with him.

"I bet he does," she laughed placing Carter on her hip. "He probably wants me to finish the steaks while he plays with Carter. He knows that I've to get up early for work tomorrow. Since I graduated from college last week and I'm on staff at the hospital as a doctor now, my hours are crazy." Traci went around them and headed for his brother.

"I finally have you all to myself," he whispered, hugging Cherise's body to his.

"Why are you doing this to me? We have been over this."

"No, you have given me orders that I never agreed to," he corrected. "Now, let's go for that walk." Spinning Cherise in his arms, Lee linked his fingers with her and led her in the direction of the hidden trail.

# Chapter Twenty-One

"Tell me why you've been avoiding me all night. I think about what we have shared. I deserve a little of your attention, Ms. Roberts. I was almost getting jealous of my little brother."

"You can't be serious," Cherise laughed, shaking her head at him. "I was only talking to Brad. He's so sweet and so in love with Alicia. I hope she comes to her senses and sees what a great guy Brad is."

"Why don't you take some of your own advice?"

"What are you talking about?" Cherise asked. "I'm not confused about my feelings about anyone."

Taking Cherise by the hand, Lee escorted her over to a rosebush by an iron seat. He waited until she took a seat and then joined her. He was ready to get all of this out in the open. "Cherise, I care a lot about you. I want to spend all the time with you I can. I love how you think and I want to learn more about you. Tell me about your childhood and what you dreamt about being as a little girl."

"Lee…"

"How about for once you just say 'yes' and see how things turn out. Don't you think it's time that you stop living in the past? I'm not going to hurt you, Cherise. I want to show you how nice I can be, but you have to give me a chance."

Lee waited while the scent of the roses surrounded them and the sound of crickets and the other night creatures moved around in the dark. He just opened up his heart to Cherise and he prayed with everything in him that she didn't toss it back at him.

"I'll try," Cherise said so low that he thought he might not have heard it.

"Are you saying that you're going to go out with me?"

"Yes. I'll see where this can go between the two of us. I'm tired of allowing my past to rule my future."

Cupping Cherise's face in his hands, he planted a long kiss on her mouth. "I swear you won't regret this. I'm going to make you so happy. Can you just do me one little favor?"

"What is it?" she asked, wrapping her arms around his neck.

"Stop hanging around David so much at work. I know that he has a wife, but every time I see him with you I get so damn jealous."

"You being jealous of David is so funny," Cherise chuckled. "He's totally in love with Mary. He doesn't think of me like that. David was trying to set me up on a blind date a while back."

"I know and I wasn't happy about it, either." Lee picked Cherise up and placed her on his thighs. "I want to rip the guy's eyes out for even looking at you. You're mine and I don't share."

"I'm too heavy for you," Cherise complained, squirming on his lap. She tried to move back to her seat, but he stopped her.

"Will you stop with the weight issues? I find all of you beautiful and I don't know how you can't see it. Your curves are meant for me and no one else." He ran his hands down the front of Cherise's dress and stopped at her breast. "I could get lost in these beauties. Sometimes I dream about sucking them all night long. Do you want me to do that tonight?"

"We can't get into this out here. Someone may come looking for us."

"Are you saying we can get into it later tonight?" Lee asked. "I miss having you in my bed."

"You're too much. Can you ever think about something else?" Cherise inquired.

"Can you blame me for wanting to make love to the woman I love?"

Lee realized his mistake before Cherise jumped off of him. "Don't do that. You can't be in love with me."

He saw the fear in her eyes and it pained him that her ex-boyfriend made her not believe in love anymore. He was going to make sure that she took the love he offered her. "Sunshine, I'm in love with you and I'm not afraid to tell you. I can understand that you're nervous about this, but I can wait until you're confident enough to tell me the words." Reaching out, he grabbed Cherise's wrist and pulled her back down on his lap.

"Lee, this is too much for me right now. I'm beginning to accept that the views I had in the past were wrong. My life has changed so much in these past couple of months and I'm trying to piece all of it together. I don't believe I can find the love Traci has with your brother. I'm too jaded for that."

"Sweetheart, there's nothing wrong with having a little fear, but don't let it hold you back from what you feel for me. I'm not asking you to give up who you are. I just want you to make a place for me in your heart. Do you think that you can do that?"

"I want to."

"Good, that's all you have to say," Lee whispered by her ear. "Let's take this like a getting-to-know-you period. We can go out on dates and learn more about each other. I know there's something you're dying to ask me about."

"There are some things I do want to ask you about," Cherise confessed.

"See? I knew it. How about tomorrow after work I take you out to dinner and you can dig deep into my past?"

"Are you going to be honest?"

"I have no reason to lie to the woman I'm falling in love with." Before Cherise could correct him, Lee planted a quick kiss on her mouth. "We better get back before your sister comes looking for us. I think Traci believes I'm trying to seduce you into marrying me." Lee lifted Cherise off his body and placed her in front of him.

Cherise's heart jumped at Lee's words. "Are you?"

Wrapping his arm around her waist, he winked down at her and led her back in the direction of the house. "I'll never tell."

# Chapter Twenty-Two

The way the jeans were hugging her ass almost made him forget the reason he came into the kitchen. Easing up behind her, Lee wrapped his arms around Cherise's waist and tugged her back against his chest. "What are you doing?" He glanced over her shoulder at all of the cookbooks spread across the kitchen counter.

"I'm trying to come up with a new recipe for the party I'm catering this weekend," Cherise answered, resting her hands on his arms.

"I can think of something I want to get all fired up," he growled while nibbling at the back of her neck.

"You stay fired up," Cherise laughed, wiggling out of his arms. "I don't have time to fool around. This is a very important party. If I do well, this might set me up as being one of the best caterers in town."

"You're already the best caterer in the state. You don't need this guy to tell you that." Lee hated how stressed this event was making Cherise. He was noticing how the pressure was making her lose weight and he wasn't pleased.

"How about you stop working on this and let me take you out to dinner? We haven't been out on a date yet since we decided to become a couple."

"Oh, I can't do that. I want to get everything laid out so when I talk to Simon tomorrow I'll be prepared."

"Simon can wait," Lee said. Going over to Cherise, he grabbed her by the hand and took her out of the kitchen.

"There's a new Chinese place I want to try and I'm not going to take no for an answer."

* * * *

"Don't you think Richard might be upset we didn't go to *D4*?" Cherise asked, then took a bite of her shrimp egg roll.

"He doesn't care I didn't go to the restaurant tonight. I think he has bigger problems on his hands at the moment with Dawn."

"What's wrong with them? I thought they were madly in love with each other."

"Oh, they are. But Richard is ready to get married and I think Dawn is having cold feet about it," Lee answered.

"I can understand that. Marriage is a big step and if you aren't prepared for it, then a person shouldn't get married."

"So, you're agreeing with Dawn. You think she should keep playing this hot and cold game with my brother's feelings? Isn't that unfair to him? He's madly in love with her and wants to make a life with her, but she's too scared to let him."

"How do you know that Dawn doesn't want to marry Richard? Maybe it's something else that is making her say no. Has Richard taken the time to see past Dawn's saying no to see what the real problem may be? Could there be something else that is holding her back?"

"What are you taking about? Are you saying that my brother is selfish and only wants his way?" Wiping her mouth with a napkin, Cherise shook her head at him. "No, I'm not saying that, but the Drace men do have a way of not taking no for an answer."

"Can you blame us for fighting for something that we want?" Lee inquired.

"No, I can't. I'm just saying that Richard needs to see what the underlying problem is about with Dawn not wanting to get married. I think they're a beautiful couple. I can see how much they love each other."

"Would you marry me if I asked you?" Lee tossed out, shocking Cherise.

Surprise, shock and utter disbelief were the emotions that passed over Cherise's face while he waited for a response. He didn't know what she would say to him, but it wasn't looking good. Surely, she wasn't that clueless about how he felt about her.

"I'm not ever going to get married. I made that decision a long time ago."

"You wouldn't marry me or any man?"

"I would tell another man the same answer," she replied.

"Even a black man?" Lee couldn't help it, he had to ask.

"What does a black man have to do with this?"

He wasn't going to let her sit there and pretend like she didn't know what he was talking about. "It wasn't too long ago that you swore you would only date a black man and then I forced my way into your life. I'm only wondering if you would tell a black man the same answer."

"You can't be serious. I thought I told you how wrong I was about believing those things. Are you still holding that against me?" Lee tried not to remember how Cherise was in the past, but it was still there in the back of his mind. For a long time, she hated that Traci was with his brother. She even confronted him on several occasions about it. How could he not think she would be more excited about marrying a black man instead of him?

"I guess a part of me is just wondering whether you would tell someone who wasn't white no."

"Do you know how stupid this conversation is?" Cherise demanded. "I thought we were coming out to spend some time with each other. However, you decided to bring stuff up from the past."

"You didn't answer my question," he tossed back.

"Lee, drop it. I don't want to go into this anymore. It's stupid."

"Cherise, you've answered my question," he snapped angrily. Standing up, he shook his head at the woman who was slowly breaking his heart. "I'm going to pay for the meal and then I'll be waiting for you in the car." Lee stormed away without giving Cherise a chance to say a word to him.

The ride home was filled with tense silence. Neither one wanted to express what was on their minds. Cherise took a peek at Lee from the corner of her eye and she noticed how hard his jaw was clenched. How could Lee think she would be interested in dating a black man when she was so in love with him? Was he really that insecure?

God, he was all that she thought about now. She loved waking up in the middle of the night with his arms wrapped around her. She was even starting not to think about her body concerns anymore. Maybe it was time that she told him how she felt. He had been so patient waiting for her. She could see how he might think she wasn't interested in making a life with him.

Cherise waited until Lee pulled into the driveway and shut off the car before she tried to talk to him. "Lee, I need to tell you something." She reached out and touched him on the arm, but he shook off her hand.

"Cherise, I'm not in the mood for this tonight. I'm going to have a busy day at the office tomorrow, so I won't be at Crane's. You're going to have to work on the presentation by yourself. Also, I think it might be best if we slept in separate rooms tonight." Once again, he left her sitting alone as he got out of the car, unlocked the front door and went inside the house.

She wouldn't let Lee see how much his words had hurt her. If he wanted to get pissed over something stupid, then let him. She didn't have the time to stroke his ego. He was the one who jumped to the wrong conclusion and he could be the one who apologized later.

# *Chapter Twenty-Three*

"You look awfully busy. What are you doing here this late? Usually you're gone by now. Is there something going on I should know about?" David asked her from the opened doorway.

Cherise laid a paper to the side and glanced at David over her glasses. "I'm working on the presentation that I'm assigned to with Lee. I want everything to look perfect for it."

"Yeah, I heard something about an online magazine or something like that?"

"Some thing like that," she smiled and then dropped her eyes back down to the layout pages in front of her. "So, why are you here this late? I thought Mary was coming back into town."

"She came back last night and she is working on a new song. I can't believe how much time she spends in the studio. Sometimes I think she loves her backup singers more than me."

"You aren't serious, are you?"

"No, I'm not. Mary is totally in love with me. How could she not be? I'm so handsome," David boasted.

"Handsome, yes, but modest, no," Cherise teased back. "How are things going with you? You stay so busy I haven't had a chance to talk to you lately."

"Everything is good. Work is busy as usual, but you know that. Missy hasn't been bothering me and I think I might get another account from Mr. Crane pretty soon."

"Excellent, I'm glad you're doing well." David heard the sadness in Cherise's voice and he knew something was wrong with his friend. "Okay, tell me what is wrong," he said, coming into the room. "I can hear you're upset about something."

"It's nothing. I can handle it." She didn't want to get into her personal life with David.

"Cherise, we're friends and I'm here for you. Just tell me what is wrong. Is it Lee?"

Cherise took her glasses off and tossed them to the side. She wanted to talk to someone, but she always couldn't take her problems to Traci since she was married to Zack now. She liked her brother-in-law, but he was Lee's brother and eventually her conversation would get back to him.

"Lee and I are having a small disagreement," she admitted.

"Business or personal," David asked, shocking her.

"How did you know we were dating?"

"I have eyes. I notice how he can't take his eyes off you anytime you enter a room. I think the two of you make a good-looking couple."

"Lee said that I'm his soul mate, but I'm not so sure."

"Cherise, you have to stop thinking about stuff so much and just go with the flow. Lee is so perfect for you, but if you keep pushing him away. You might lose him."

"Why do you think it's my fault?"

"Can I tell you something and you promise not to get upset?" David came across the room and took a seat at the table with her. "I think we're good enough friends that I can be honest with you."

"You know how much I love honesty."

"Yes, you love to give people your honest opinion, but are you strong enough to take it?"

She knew David was trying to push her buttons and he was succeeding in getting what he wanted. What could

136

he tell her that she already didn't know about herself? "Sure, give it to me. I can take it."

"Remember that you told me to tell you this."

Cherise was tried of David stepping around the subject. "Spit it out."

"You're scared of giving your heart to someone. You come off like this ice princess type that doesn't need anyone to hold her hand or tell her how beautiful she looks, but you do. Lee figured that out about you and it scared the shit out of you. You have to let someone in your heart or it's going to be so closed off that you'll never be able to do it."

"When did you become a relationship therapist?" Cherise teased, trying not to listen to the words David was telling her.

"I was like you and it almost cost me Mary. I love her so much and I couldn't see my life without her in it. Now, you have to think about Lee and your real feelings for him. Are you willing to live your life without him? Or are you strong enough to see where it could go with him?"

Cherise hated that David sounded like her sister and Lee. Why did everyone think Lee was the *perfect* man for her? Sure when she was around him, it felt right, but he did get on her nerves at times, too. Lee had all the qualities she was looking for in a man, but she was scared to give her heart to him.

"I just don't know."

"How about for once you go with the flow and see where it leads you? You might be surprised at the outcome."

She had missed Lee and his wicked sense of humor. "Okay, I'll talk to him tonight when I get home."

"Why are you going to wait until tonight when he's in his office right now?" David asked.

Cherise couldn't keep the surprise out of her voice. "What? How long has he been here? I thought he was at his own work place."

"I saw him coming from the stairs when I was on my way here. I'm pretty sure he didn't see me. He looked like he was deep in thought. So, are you going to talk to him?"

Apprehension worked its way into Cherise's body, but she shoved it down. She needed to talk to Lee and now was as good as time as any. "Yes, I am."

"Good, I am tired of seeing that sad look on your face," David said as he headed for the door. "Remember, you can't let his ego get in the way. Lee is probably still upset about whatever your last conversation was with him. Don't let him push you away." David's words hung in the air long after he had left her alone.

Cherise gathered up all the layouts she was working on and shoved them into her attaché case. Grabbing her purse off the back of her chair, she made her way out of her office and headed for Lee's. He wasn't going to get the last word this time. She had something to say and he was going to listen to her.

\* \* \* \*

Taking off his tie, Lee tossed it on his table and undid the first two buttons on his shirt. He had no reason to be here late as it was, but he wasn't ready to go home and see Cherise. She has been trying to talk to him and he has been shoving her away. He felt bad for jumping on her like he did, but the words were out of his mouth before he could stop them.

Why couldn't he just enjoy the time he had with Cherise? Instead, he tried to force something that wasn't there. She said she was willing to give them a chance as a couple and he tossed it back in her face. Yet, she didn't understand that he was more than a little worried that a strong black man would come along and steal her away from him. Cherise could toss him to the side without a second thought. He wasn't ready to let her go. She was the perfect woman for him and she was too willful to admit it.

"Why can't I have any luck with her?" Lee asked himself out loud.

"Who are you trying to have luck with?" A soft voice inquired from behind him.

Looking away from the window and the street below, Lee glanced over his shoulder and found the object of his affection standing directly by the edge of his desk. Cherise was looking breathtaking in a peach dress. It showed off all of her curves and his cock stood up at attention. Making him remember how long it had been since he had made love to the beautiful woman behind him.

"What are you doing here? I thought you would be at the house?"

"I was working late on the magazine presentation," Cherise replied, tossing her belongings down in a chair. "I was surprised to find out that you were here."

"I wanted some quiet to think about some things," Lee answered, folding his arms over his chest.

"I can only guess what is going on in that head of yours."

"I won't lie. I was thinking about us and how you won't give me a chance. I'm tired of being the one who is trying to make something happen here," he admitted.

"Lee, I was trying to give you a chance the other day on our date, but you stormed inside the house. I haven't been able to get you alone since there." Cherise came across the room and stopped in front of him. "I've been thinking about us too lately and I want to get some things off my chest."

Lee slowly prepared himself for the worst because he knew Cherise wasn't ready to give him a chance. She had too much baggage from her past to get over first. She would never know how to love because she wasn't able to let her heart heal.

MARIE ROCHELLE

"I already know what you're going to tell me," Lee confessed, uncrossing his arms.

One perfectly trimmed eyebrow arched over Cherise's eyes. "Oh, you do. How can you be so sure?"

"It's constantly the same thing. You want me to stay out of your life. Despite the fact we're ideal for each our and the sex is out of this world, you're going to deny everything and go back into that cocoon that you hide in."

"Mr. Drace, if you were a betting man, you would be in the poor house," Cherise laughed. Stepping closer, she wrapped her arms around his neck. "Lee, I'm falling in love with you. I didn't think it was possible, but it is. I love being around you and I wasn't happy when I didn't get to see your face every morning. I don't want any other man but you. How about we shove our past behind us and see where this can go?"

"Are you sure?" Lee asked as he grabbed her ass and yanked her close. "I'm going to give this relationship all that I have and if you aren't, let's end it before it begins."

"I'm tired of running from what I feel for you. So sorry, but I'm not going anywhere," Cherise smiled, then planted a kiss on his mouth.

"Damn, how quick do you think we can get home? I got a lot of making up to do with you," he growled in her ear as he rubbed his erection against her stomach.

"I know. I won't be able to make it all the way to your house. How about we stop at the hotel and make a night of it? It's Friday, so we can check in for the weekend and leave late Sunday?" Cherise suggested as her fingers played with the buttons on his shirt.

"I'm mad I didn't think of it," he whispered before capturing Cherise's mouth with his.

# *Chapter Twenty-Four*

"I never thought the two of them would get married," Cherise said, taking a sip of her champagne as Richard danced with Dawn in front of them. The place was packed with friends and family. A part of her wondered would she ever have enough courage to take that huge step like Dawn did.

"I know," Lee agreed, wrapping his arm around her waist. "However, Richard wasn't going to give up getting a ring on Dawn's finger. They were so in love with each other that marriage was only the next step."

"She does look so in love with him. I remember all of the fights that they used to have. It's amazing this is how their relationship ended."

"See? Sometimes all that arguing is hiding an intense passion between two people. I wonder who else might have a wedding in their future," Lee breathed by her ear as he pulled her closer to his side.

"Brad and Alicia look pretty cozy over on the patio. So, I might think they'll be the next ones going down the aisle."

"Are you trying to push me over the edge? You know that I wasn't talking about them," Lee said, taking the glass out of her hand and placing it on a tray as a waiter went past.

"Who are you talking about then?" Cherise asked, peeking at Lee from the corner of her eye.

"Cherise, you know who I am referring to, but I'm going to leave it alone for now because I don't want to ruin my brother's day. However, this isn't over between us. We're going to talk about this later."

"Now, I'm going over to wish the happy couple congratulations and then get a dance with the bride." Kissing her on the cheek, Lee walked away from her, leaving her alone with her thoughts.

Was she ready to say yes if Lee proposed to her? Everything had been so great between them since they made up his office and then spent the weekend at the hotel. He even helped her out at the catering party that she had for Simon yesterday. But, did that mean she was ready to take the big leap down the aisle with him?

The sound of her phone ringing brought her out of her thoughts. Going out into the hallway of the reception hall, she answered the phone.

"Hello?"

"Ms. Roberts, it's Doug Phipps, the plumber. I have good news for you. All of the parts I ordered came in last week and everything is installed. You can move back in when you are ready. I apologize for it taking so long. I didn't have a clue the manufacture would have to special order the parts."

"I understand since the house is so old," she answered trying to stay calm over her breaking heart. It was going to be so hard to leave Lee after living with him for so long.

"I want to thank you for calling me and I'll be at your office to pay you sometime this week."

"Not a problem. I'll be out of town at a convention until Monday. So, how about you come to my office later on in the week and pay me then. It's the least I can do since you had to wait six extra weeks for that missing piece."

"Okay, I'll see you then," Cherise replied and then disconnected the phone call.

What in the hell was she going to do now? Lee wasn't going to be happy. He was beginning to think of his house as their home and now she was about to move out. "How do I tell him?" she whispered out loud.

"Tell who what?" Lee's deep voice asked behind her.

Twirling around, Cherise pushed a strand of her away from her mouth. She might as well tell him now, because telling him later wasn't going to change anything. "That was the plumber on the phone. My house is ready for me to move back into this weekend."

"No. I wouldn't let you leave me. Things are finally going good with us and if you move back home, you'll place that wall back up."

"Lee, you knew that me staying at your house wasn't a permanent situation for my problem. I was eventually going to move back into my own place," Cherise said, trying to reason with him.

"See, I guess I wasn't thinking the same thing as you. I thought you wanted something permanent from me," Lee sighed, shaking his head. "Once again I gave you my heart on a platter and you tossed it back in my face. Well, I'm done. You win."

Cherise's heart started pounding in her chest at Lee's words. What was he saying to her? Was he tossing her to the side? Was he giving up on them because she wanted to move back home? "I'm not following you," she whispered.

"Let me explain it to you. I'm not chasing after you anymore. I've told you that I was falling in love with you. Hell, I even hinted that I wanted to marry you and none of it phased you. So, I'm done with all of it. I'm going to let you move back home without trying to stop you. Plus, after this project is over, we can go our separate ways and just be in-laws like you always wanted. I might be in love with you, but I'm tired of having my heart ripped apart." Lee gave her one long lingering look and then spun away from her. He moved back in the direction of the wedding reception.

"Lee, wait. We can talk about this," she yelled after him, but he kept going and never looked back at her.

Right at that moment, Cherise realized how much she truly loved the man that was walking away from her. "I can't lose him. I have to find a way to get him back and prove my love for him all at the same time."

CLOSER TO YOU: LEE

# Chapter Twenty-Five

"Are you sure that you really want to do this? Everything is going so good with everyone. Why ruin it with this stupidity?" Lee checked his reflection in the mirror one last time as he listened to Richard give him a lecture. He was going out on a date with Amanda and he didn't have time for this. Cherise wasn't going to give him the time of day, so it was time he moved on. She had moved out two days ago and hadn't spoken to him since. It was like she never spent all those weeks here with him. He couldn't give his heart to her anymore only to have it tossed back at him.

Amanda enjoyed his company so he was going to give it to her. "Why are you in my business anyway? Shouldn't you be home with that new wife? Does Dawn know you're here butting into my business?" Walking further into the room, Richard shook his head. "Dawn was the one who sent me over her. She's stunned that would go out on a date with another woman when you're in love with Cherise."

"I'm not in love with Cherise," Lee denied, trying to forget how it felt to have her in his life. "She's family and that is as far as it going to go between us. She constantly told me that and now I believe her."

"Man, stop being like this. Go to Cherise and tell her how you feel. You knew that she would be a hard nut to crack, but don't give up on her. Because if you lose the woman you love, you'll regret it."

"Richard, I'm very happy that you and Zack got the women that you wanted, but Cherise is different. She's isn't swayed by sweet words and flowers. I'm tired of fighting the uphill battle. She has won. I'm moving on." Zack checked his tie one last time in the mirror and then moved away. "Now, you should leave because I need to go and pick up Amanda. I can't stay out that long because I have that PowerPoint presentation tomorrow at work with Cherise."

"Why aren't you helping her with it instead of going out with Amanda?" Richard questioned, a slight frown to his face.

"Like always, Ms. Roberts informed me that she didn't need my help, so I let her have it. She's a smart woman so I know she can do it by herself," Zack replied and then walked out his bedroom door with his brother behind him.

* * * *

Cherise watched the PowerPoint presentation and wondered for a fourth time could she go through with it. This would be so out of character for her, but she had to show Lee that she could do this. He had tried talking to her since Richard's wedding, but she had been blowing him off. She had things to think about. Having him in her face would have coaxed her into doing something she wasn't ready for, but now she was.

It had taken a long time for her to get to this stage in her life. She never thought it could happen to her, however it did and she wasn't about to toss it away anymore. She hadn't even talked to Traci about this first, because she didn't want Lee to get wind of it. She wanted Lee's complete surprise. This was something he wasn't going to be ready for. Hell, she wasn't a hundred percent positive that she was ready for it either.

"I can do this. Don't get scared now. I've always been a take-charge person and this time isn't going to be any different. Tomorrow is going to change the rest of my life forever and I hope that I'm truly ready for it."

\* \* \* \*

The next day, Cherise stood in the back and watched how fast the conference room was filling up. Since she and Lee were giving the presentation, the first two seats at the table were saved for them. However, Lee wasn't here yet. The butterflies in her stomach were about to make her sick. She silently prayed that Lee showed up today and he wasn't still mad at her about what happened at Richard's wedding.

Her fingers fiddled with the necklace around her neck as she tried to calm the last of her nerves. Where was Lee? Why wasn't he here yet? Just as she was about to leave and give him a call, Lee strolled through the door with Missy close behind him. The young woman smirked in her direction and took a seat at the table next to David.

Lee paused by his seat and looked at her before he sat down. "Good morning, Cherise," he said. "Are you about ready to start this meeting?"

"Good morning, Lee," she answered, trying to stay calm. "Yes, I am. I have everything ready. I was just waiting for you to arrive."

"I'm here now, so why don't we get this started. I can't wait to see how you put our ideas together."

"Okay, let's get this started," Cherise leaned over the laptop and got the presentation ready, hoping she wasn't making the biggest mistake of her life.

Turning around, she moved to the side and watched as the screen in front of her started to count down and her work appeared. Cherise tried to block out the images before her, but everything was there in color. Her co-workers heads slowly turned in her direction as everyone figured out what was taking place. She only focused her attention to the words coming out of her mouth on the big screen at the head of the room.

*Lee, I know that I haven't been the most loving woman to get to know. However, you stuck with me and for that, I'll always be grateful. You're a wonderful man. I love you more than I could have though possible. Will you marry me?*

Her heart pounded in the middle of her heart as her fingers froze the picture of herself in the PowerPoint presentation. She turned slowly and looked at Lee. She didn't know how to read the look on his face. It was a mixture of disbelief and another emotion that she couldn't quite read.

Lee glanced at her and then back at the screen several times without saying a word. She didn't know if she should be excited or nervous about his lack of response. He was always so verbal when it came to her, now he wasn't speaking a word to her.

"Lee, will you marry me?" she asked, moving a little closer to his chair. Cherise could feel her face growing hotter as everyone stared at her then back at Lee. He was really putting her on the spot.

It seemed like it took forever before Lee stood up in front of her. He opened his mouth like he was going to answer her, but instead he snapped it shut and brushed past her. She stood in silence and watched Lee as he left her alone and utterly embarrassed in front of her co-workers.

Cherise held her tears at bay as she laid the remote on the table and left with room with several pairs of eyes burning a hole into her back. She opened her heart up to Lee and he stomped on it without a second thought. How was she ever going to be able to look at him in the eye again without living this moment over and over again? No, she had to find a way to distance herself away from him and the sooner the better.

# *Chapter Twenty-Six*

"Cherise, you can't be serious!" Traci snapped in the phone. "Why don't you come over here and we can talk about this."

"No. I can't face anyone at work after what happened. Hell, I do have a little pride left. Besides I've already turned in the real PowerPoint to Mr. Cane along with my letter of registration. He wasn't happy, but he took it." Cherise didn't want to hear a lecture from her baby sister. She wasn't going to call Traci at all until Simon talked her into it. "This is a wonderful opportunity for me. I'm glad Simon came to my house and asked me. I don't have anything here to make me stay."

"What about me and Carter?" Traci demanded. "You know how much he loves his Aunt Cherise. You've got to stop running every time something goes wrong."

"Traci, I proposed to Lee in front of everyone I worked with," she snapped over the phone. "He didn't even have enough class to tell me no. He just got up and walked out on me. Do you know how that made me feel?"

"Cherise, Lee is an idiot. But that doesn't mean you have to travel half way around the world to get away from him. Come over here to my house and we can discuss this."

Cherise wanted Traci to understand that she wasn't going back home for a long time. Simon loved her cooking skills so much that he offered her a job as his personal chef in Paris and she took it. Lee would be out of her life forever and it was for the best. She should have listened to her mind at first instead of allowing him to worm his way into her heart.

"Traci, you know that I love you, but I'm not coming back. Please just box up the things in my house and I'll take care of the rest of the details."

"No, I'm not going to do that. I'm coming to that airport and I'm going to bring you back here. I'll drag you back kicking and screaming if I have to," Traci threatened.

"Honey, it's too late. I'm already on the plane with Simon. I'm just talking to you while he finishes talking with the pilot. Please don't be upset because I'm not. How many caterers get to live out their cooking dreams in Paris?"

"I love you and I'll get in touch with you after I get settled in." Cherise quickly hung up the phone before Traci could talk her into staying. She wasn't ready to go another round with her sister about this. She was on her way to Paris and there was nothing Traci or anyone else could do to stop her.

* * * *

Traci snapped the phone shut and flung it down on the table. "This is all your fault," she yelled at the man at the head of the table. "If you hadn't broken her heart, she wouldn't have left."

Lee leaned back in his chair and stared at her with a clueless expression on his face. "Traci, I don't know what you're talking about. What did I do?"

"You know what you did, you bastard," she hissed. "You left my sister standing there after she proposed to you and now she's gone and never coming back. I encouraged her to give you a chance when she didn't want to. Why didn't I listen to her? You are a waste of skin and I hope you get what you deserve."

"Sweetheart, what's wrong?" Zack asked, touching her on the arm, but she jerked away from his touch.

"Don't you touch me!" Traci jerked her arm away from her husband and stood up. "I'm going upstairs to get Carter and then I'm out of here." Walking over to Lee, she gave him a hard look. "You should be happy to know that my sister accepted a job in Paris as a personal chef. She just told me on the phone to box up her stuff because she has no reason to come back home."

"Cherise wouldn't leave without letting me know," Lee whispered, looking at her. "She couldn't have run away like that."

"What reason did you give her to stay? She opened her heart and let you in. Do you know how much courage it took for her to admit her feelings in front of everyone? Cherise had always been such a private person and she let that go for you. You never loved my sister."

"I love Cherise," Lee answered. "I'm in love with her."

"Sure you are and that's why you didn't accept her marriage proposal," Traci accused. "I have to leave before I say something I might regret later." Turning, she hurried in the direction of the stairs when Zack's voice stopped her.

"I'll be up in a few minutes to help you with Carter."

"No, don't. I need some time alone and seeing you right now isn't going to help my opinion of Lee. Why don't you stay here with him tonight? I'm going to spend the night at Cherise's house anyway." Without waiting for Zack to respond, Traci disappeared upstairs.

Zack sat in his seat torn between going after his wife and beating the hell out of his dumb-ass brother. How could Lee do that to Cherise? Didn't he warn Lee months ago about breaking Cherise's heart? Now Traci was upset at Lee and he was getting pulled into the mess.

"Look what you have done," Zack snapped. "Why in the hell did you do that to Cherise? She finally let down her defenses and admitted to being in love with you. How did you repay her? You tossed her love back in her face. God, man, do you have a brain injury or something?"

"I got scared," Lee confessed. "Cherise was offering me everything I wanted after so long and her proposal threw me. I was going to apologize, but I didn't think she would see me. You know how stubborn she can be. I never thought she would run off to Paris with some man. I'll bet money that Simon was the one who offered her the job."

"So, are you going to let her get away from you?" Zack questioned. "You need to fix this because I'm not going to have Traci mad at me. I love my family and I'm not going to lose them because of you."

The sound of Traci coming downstairs drew Zack attention. He watched as Traci paused in the middle of the living room and looked at him. He wanted to run over there and tell her not to leave, but he understood that she needed this time to herself with their son.

"I'll come by Cherise's tomorrow with breakfast and we can take Carter to the park," he suggested.

"Okay. That sounds nice," Traci agreed and then she looked at Lee. "You better find a way to get my sister to come back home or you will wish that you had." Spinning on her heel, Traci left the house, slamming the door behind her.

"Cherise hates me now. There's no way she's going to listen to a word that I've to say. She'll probably have me tossed out before the words *I'm sorry* leave my mouth," Lee sighed, running his fingers through his hair.

"Do you really love Cherise?" Zack asked. "I mean is she the last person you think about before you go to bed? Is her name the first word that leaves your mouth when you wake up in the morning?"

"Of course. I think about her every waking moment of the day. I don't know what I'm going to do without her in my life. Shit, I only went out with Amanda to get over the pain of her rejection. What's so funny is she was all I talked about all night and Amanda understood. She sat there and let me vent."

"Big brother, I guess you better find out the earliest flight you can get to Paris because Cherise isn't coming back home unless you give her a damn good reason. That woman risked everything and proposed to you and you tossed it to the side. I just hope you haven't ruined your chances at getting her back," Zack said. "Paris is a romantic city and Cherise is a good-looking woman. I'm sure some Frenchman would love to snatch her up and make her his."

"Cherise is mine," Lee growled as he jumped up from the table. "I'm not going to share the woman I love with anyone. She wants to get married and I'm going to be the only man she says 'I do' to."

"You have no claim on her. Cherise left you and she's a single, attractive woman in Paris. I know she'll find a way to push you to the back of her mind," Zack tossed back.

"She better get that idea out of her head. I'm not going to lose her." Lee stated as he turned to leave the room.

"Where are you going?" Zack yelled after him

"I'm going to get my future wife back."

# Chapter Twenty-Seven

*Paris, France*
*Two weeks later*

"Why are you out in on the terrace instead of inside enjoying the party? The food is out of this world. I've gotten so many compliments about how this is the best get-together I've had in years," Simon said, standing next to her.

"I'm glad that everything is to your liking," Cherise answered. "I just wanted some time alone to think about things." She loved being here in Paris, but she was a little home sick. All of her family was there and she missed Traci and Carter.

"Drace is a fool to let you slip through his fingers. You're a gorgeous woman," Simon said, standing next to her. "I would love to have a beautiful and intelligent woman in love with me."

Cherise looked at Simon from the corner of her eye and was surprised that she wasn't attracted to him. He was everything that she had been looking for in the past. A handsome, good-looking black man, but he wasn't doing a thing for her. Most black woman would love how he looked like Jesse Martin, but his looks weren't turning her on at all.

Her heart was still stinging from how Lee ripped it out of her chest and tossed it to the side. Simon was a wonderful man, but he wasn't the man for her. Maybe after some time had passed and her soul was healed, she could look at him in a different light.

"I'm not thinking about Lee. He's in my brother-in-law and nothing more," she lied. "I don't have those kinds of feelings for him."

"You need to stop lying to yourself," Simon stated. "I saw how the two of you looked at each other at that party you catered for me. I know two people in love when I see them."

"One thing I know for sure is that Lee doesn't love me. He loves to control the situation and have power over everyone, but he never cared about me a day in his life." Cherise shook away the memory of Lee walking away after her proposal from her mind. It was best to leave the past in the past. She was never going to see him again, so it was for the best if she got on with her life.

"Can I have a few minutes alone?"

Simon studied her for a few minutes. "I don't want you out here by yourself thinking about your life. Come back inside with me and have a glass of champagne."

"I'm not much of a drinker. I just want some time alone. I promise you that I'm not going to jump off the terrace or anything," Cherise laughed. She was hurt, but she wasn't depressed enough to do anything that stupid.

"Okay, I'll leave you alone." Simon kissed her on the cheek and then went back inside closing the door behind him.

Cherise let the warm night arm brush over her arms as she stared out into the lights shining in the dark. It was a beautiful night and she didn't have anyone to share it with. Right now, she should be planning her wedding with Lee instead of being half way across the world standing alone. Why did she let Lee into her heart? She knew that he was going to break her heart and she allowed it to happen. She had worked for years to get that wall around her emotions and Lee picked it away without a problem.

She had to be the dumbest woman in the world to fall for all of his false promises. God, he came on to her at a party that his girlfriend was having. She should have known that was the true side of him. But no, she let a few passionate kisses and amazing mind-blowing sex mess with her mind. Hell, she wasn't going to let that happen again. Lee's rejection had taught her a valuable lesson. One that she didn't need repeated for anything in this world. The sound of the patio doors opening behind her made her take a deep breath. Why couldn't Simon listen to her?

"Simon, didn't I tell you I wanted to be alone?"

"I'm not Simon," a familiar male voice answered, making the hair of the back of her neck stand up.

Cherise didn't turn around because she couldn't look at the man behind her not after what he did. "What are you doing here? How in the hell did you find me?"

"Simon helped me. I called his office and they forwarded my message to him. He talked to me the middle of last week and told me about the party," Lee answered. "Cherise, I want to talk to you. I need to explain about what happened."

"No," she snapped. "I can't believe a word that comes out of your mouth. You wasted a trip here. Go back home and forget my name."

"It's very hard to forget the woman's name you're in love with." Lee stopped behind her and brushed the hair off her shoulder.

Stepping to the side, Cherise put some distance between herself and Lee. "Don't touch me. You lost that right a long time ago."

"Sunshine, I know that I fucked up and I want to make things right between us. I love you with everything in my heart."

Spinning around, Cherise swallowed down a moan at the sight of Lee in his tuxedo. It fit his body like it had been tailor made for him. It was taking all of her will power not to touch him. "You don't care about me. So why don't you stop lying? You wanted to break through the wall of Cherise and that's what you did. Why don't you go back home and date Missy or Amanda? I think either one of them are more of your type."

"Do you know how stunning you look in that white dress tonight?" Lee asked, totally ignoring her comment. "When I saw you through the door I almost forget what I was going to say. I know you have every man here wondering if your back is as smooth as it looks. You never wore a backless dress for me before. I think I'm a little jealous."

"Lee, did you even hear what I said?"

"Yes, I heard you trying to make me date two women that I have no interest in," Lee answered as he took a step closer to her. "I don't want Missy or Amanda. I want a feisty woman that's going to fight me at every turn. I want her to have the body of a goddess with a sharp mind that will keep me on my toes."

"Well, you're looking in the wrong place because I'm not her. Because if I was, you wouldn't have run out on my proposal," Cherise countered.

"Hell, I was an idiot to do that. I just couldn't believe that you had finally opened up to me and in front of all of those people. I can admit that I got a little scared and had to leave, but baby that wasn't your fault." Lee slipped his fingers through her hair and wrapped his other hand around her waist. He slowly slid her body to his and brushed a soft kiss across her mouth. "I was thrilled that you asked me to marry you. I would love to be your husband."

"It's too late for that now," she whispered, trying to get away from Lee. However, he only tightened his grip and pulled her closer to his hard body.

"I'm not going to take your word on that. I know it isn't too late for us. When two people love each other as much as we do, passion like that doesn't die. I love you with everything I have in me and I'm going to fight to get your love back," Lee swore.

*Stay strong. Don't let his words sneak back into your heart. He dumped you like yesterday's newspaper. Lee Drace only loves one person and that's himself.* "No, this isn't going to work between us. I can't do this again."

"Cherise, I can't lose you. I want what my brothers have and I know I can find that with you," Lee whispered by her ear.

"What are you talking about?" she leaned back in Lee's arms and stared up into his eyes. She loved how big and strong he was. She always felt so petite in his embrace. It was going to hurt not being a part of his life anymore.

"Zack and Richard found the loves of their lives and without a doubt you're the love of my life. Have you ever noticed how they can look at their wives across the room and know what they are thinking? I want that connection with you. When I have a problem at work, I want to come home and discuss it with my gorgeous wife.

"I want to be the one you come to when you can't figure out a recipe or you just want to vent about Missy at work. God, I'm so jealous of the relationship you have with David. He's like your best friend and I hate that. Do you know how many times I would watch the two of you interact with each other and wish it was me in his place? Don't you understand that you're my everything?"

"Lee, we just aren't good together."

"See, that's where you're wrong. We're perfect for each other. I hate to think I might have ruined any chance of us being together for the rest of our lives. Since you have been gone, my mind hasn't been able to function. All

I do is think about you and what my stupidity tossed away."

Cherise felt her heart opening up at Lee's words. She was still in love with him, but it still stung that he walked away from her proposal. "What makes you think we can have what Zack and Traci have? I don't even think we can compare ourselves to Richard and Dawn? What they have is so pure and romantic."

"You're right. We can't have what they have, because we aren't them. You're Cherise Roberts, a determined and opinionated woman who will keep me on my toes every day that we're together. I love that I never know what you're going to say or do. That is what makes you the woman I fell in love with. I wouldn't want you to be anyone else but you."

"Maybe I don't want to be with you anymore," she tossed back, trying to hold on to the last shred of her heart before she completely lost it to Lee.

"I think that you do, but you're pissed at me and I'm going to have to work my ass off to get you to love me again." Lee cupped her chin in his hand and brushed his thumbs across her lips. "Cherise, I'll do anything to prove that I'm in love with you. You're the woman I want to be with more than anything in the world. Please don't let my knee-jerk reaction keep us from being husband and wife. Baby, I truly love you and can't live without you."

"Are you going to get down on one knee and asked me to marry you?" Cherise asked, wrapping her arms around Lee's neck. "It's only fair that you propose to me this time. I'm not about to ask you again."

"Does this mean you still love me and want to spend the next fifty years with me?" Lee grinned.

"I guess I can agree to that," she smiled.

"Wonderful, we can book the next flight back home and then I can make it official in front of the entire family."

"Why do you have to wait for them?" Cherise frowned. "I'm ready to hear it now."

"They'll never believe that you allowed me to get close to you again after what happened and I want to see the look on Traci's face when you say yes."

"Do you know how much I love you?" Cherise asked as she smiled at Lee and wondered what took her so long to realize he was *the one* for her.

"It doesn't matter because I love you a hundred times more than that and I promise to prove it every day of our lives," Lee swore right before he kissed her.

# *About the Author*

Marie Rochelle is an award-winning author of erotic, interracial romance, including the Phaze titles *All the Fixin'*, *My Deepest Love: Zack*, and *Caught*. Visit her online at http://www.freewebs.com/irwriter/.

NEXT GENERATION
INDIE BOOK AWARDS

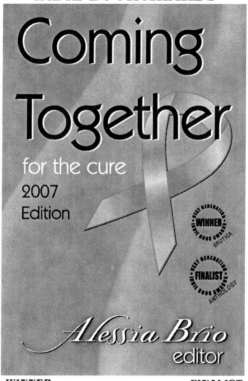

Coming
Together
for the cure
2007
Edition

Alessia Brio
editor

**WINNER**
Best Erotica

**FINALIST**
Best Anthology

**indiebookawards.com**

Printed in the United States
133853LV00001B/59/P

9 781606 590430